How My Heart Finds Christmas

by

Gail MacMillan

How My Heart Finds Christmas

Cover Art by *Tina Lynn Stout*

The Wild Rose Press, Inc.
PO Box 708
Adams Basin, NY 14410-0708
Visit us at www.thewildrosepress.com

Publishing History
First Mainstream General Edition, 2014
Digital ISBN 978-1-62830-559-3

Published in the United States of America

An occasional mutter from Steve, as we tramped along, reaffirmed he still wasn't happy with our second choice excursion.

We paused as we reached the bank above the river and suddenly…magic. Shy at first, then gradually sprouting higher and higher up among the stars in the night sky, the Northern Lights appeared. Undulating like mystic spirits gowned in green and white, they rose and rose, then doubled back on themselves to rise again. The heavens danced, alive with their essence.

I glanced down at Steve. With the dogs sitting by his side, he stared spellbound.

In the Far North, people say they've heard the Northern Lights speak in the whistling voice of migratory birds. Auroras, they claim, are sent to buoy up people's spirits during the long winter when the sun doesn't shine.

Apparently they had the same effect on my son.

"Wow!" he breathed, delighted astonishment erasing all traces of discontent.

No neon display could equal it. "Bah humbug" faded from my thoughts, the wonder that is Christmas reviving in my heart in the presence of this, truly one of nature's priceless gifts.

When the mystic dance finally began to recede, we turned and headed back to the camp. The enchanted lights of the winter night would fade from the sky but never from my memory or that of the entranced boy by my side. Those magical moments in the moonlight would live forever within us, one we could never have experienced if we hadn't made that annual Yuletide trek to the camp. Now, each year, their memory helps revive the magic of Christmas in my heart.

Dedication

To my family, whose love and generosity
have inspired so many of these stories,
and to my wonderful dogs, who have faithfully
companioned me over the years

Foreword

Each year it seems the true spirit of Christmas becomes harder and harder to find. Materialism overshadows so much of the wonder that is the genuine Yuletide reason. I'm not simply referring to the religious aspect although that is an invaluable component. What I mean is the family and friends aspect. This warm feeling of togetherness reassures us we're not alone in the universe, that there are hands and hearts willing to share our bad as well as our good times, ready to help us through the upcoming New Year with all its joys and sorrows. A hug, a smile, a few kind words can do more for us than the most expensive gift.

For the past fifteen years, I've been writing Christmas stories for various magazines. Each year as I sit down to compose yet another, I feel a pleasant warmth flood into my heart. Each year I draw on memories to inspire my tales and carry me into the true spirit of Christmas, but it was only last year I realized it was through my stories that my heart rediscovers the wonder that is Christmas, December after December.

Some ancient cultures regarded the heart as the centre of the soul. Maybe that's why it's so important each December that this life-affirming organ rediscovers Christmas for me. I hope it will continue to do so for many Yuletides to come.

A Cornucopia
of Childhood Christmas Chronicles

My earliest recollections of happy Christmases are of my father, a gifted story teller in the oral tradition, and the tales he'd weave around the Yuletide season.

For most children, classic Christmas stories include *A Christmas Carol*, *The Night before Christmas*, and *The Grinch Who Stole Christmas*. Mine were different. Among my favorite titles were *The Tale of the Crackling Christmas Tree*, *The Contrary Christmas Pony*, and *The Skater and the Wolves*.

If you have access to a New Brunswick school reader from around the beginning of the twentieth century, you might be able to locate the latter but you won't find the first two titles there or in any bookstore or library or even on the Internet. They're my father's original, until now, unpublished creations.

My father would weave tales of his boyhood Christmas Eve sleigh rides to church that crackled with all the crystalline clarity of a December frost. I could almost feel the sharp, cold air brushing my cheeks and hear the jingle of sleigh bells, the horse snorting and blowing as it lumbered along the roughly broken road.

As my father recounted the events of those evenings, I was drawn back to those times, into the frosty air and moonlight, huddled beneath dusty buffalo robes pulled into winter utilization from their summer hibernation on pegs in the stable. Excitement rushed through me in expectation of the days to come as the chestnut Percheron pulled the sleigh through the bright and drifted snow.

My father's anticipation would have been much more real and immediate. In those days, before electricity had reached their small, rural community, the church Christmas tree was illuminated by real candles. Regularly assigned the task of bucket brigade in the event, which was usually the case, the tree caught fire, my father and his four brothers would eagerly await the need for their services. When the tree finally burst into flames, the Fowlie boys had the responsibility of extinguishing the conflagration. It was the highlight of their Christmas Eve celebrations

My father and his brothers, in spite of being entrusted with this seemingly adult responsibility, weren't so different from kids today. They, too, had Christmas wish lists. Granted, the items weren't as numerous, expensive, or hi-tech as they've become in this new millennium but still costly and not always possible given their farm family income and the economics of the day. They asked for skate screws to fasten blades to their boots so they could go gliding across the millpond below their home. The luxury of oranges and store bought candy were hopefully added to the list. And like many kids today, they longed for a means of transportation.

Oh, nothing as grand as a bicycle. Too young to be given access to one of the farm horses, they asked for a pony.

The first Christmas after they made their request, their wish came…at least partially…true. They received a small sled, a set of mini-harness…and a bull calf.

"We did manage to wrestle him into the harness and get him attached to the sled," my father recalled. "But then he took off bucking and kicking. It took all five of us to catch him."

The brothers decided to try a new strategy. They'd take him down onto the ice of the millpond. There he wouldn't be able to gain traction on the glassy surface, rendering him manageable.

The idea, like so many others, while sounding good in theory, didn't prove out in fact. Once on the pond ice the little bull slipped, fell, then lay sprawled and inert, terrified on this foreign footing.

Struggling to get the animal back on his hooves and keep him there, the five children shoved him ashore where his objection to the harness immediately resurfaced. Dodging thrashing hooves and a swinging head, they battled him up the hill to the barn. After the panting creature had bucked his way back into his stall, the boys unanimously agreed to retire him from a career in transportation.

Undaunted, the brothers renewed their request for a pony the following Christmas. This time their wish came true. Christmas week a sturdy brown pony appeared in the stable. Excited, they harnessed it, attached it to the sled the bull calf had failed to manage, and headed out for a drive.

And drive and even ride they did…until spring arrived. The first day after warming weather melted the snow cover from the wooden bridge that led across the brook between the farm and the main community road, an unanticipated problem reared its head. It happened one sunny April morning.

My father had decided to visit a school friend on the other side of the brook. Innocently he mounted Christmas Pony and trotted out of the farmyard.

As they headed down the dirt road away from the farm, my father, a typical eleven-year-old, longed for the excitement of speed. Clucking to Christmas Pony and using his heels, he urged the little animal to an all-out run.

Wild with the joy of the pace, my father paid little heed to the bridge ahead. It was to prove a major mistake.

The moment the pony's hooves hit the bare boards of the bridge, it shrieked, reared, and bucked in such a sudden sequence, my father was tossed clear over its head.

Farm boy tough, he scrambled to his feet. Looking back to the spot from which he'd been propelled, he saw Christmas Pony standing at the edge of the boards. Ears pricked, it gazed round-eyed at its former rider as if as much surprised by the chain of events as he was. Apparently, my father deduced, Christmas Pony had been terrified by the echoing of his hooves on bare planks. Not easily deterred, he began to try to fathom a solution to the problem.

Fording the stream swollen with a spring freshet beneath the bridge definitely wasn't an option, so home my father went to enlist the assistance of his brothers. En masse the five youngsters returned to the bridge determined to make the little animal overcome its phobia.

They pushed, prodded, and pulled but it soon became apparent that nothing short of carrying Christmas Pony bodily over the boards would induce it to the far side of the brook. The boys were forced to accept the fact that whenever the bridge was bare and the stream beneath it too deep to ford, they'd once again be travelling *á pied*.

Then there was the story of the Christmas when my father, as a teenager, went a-wooing and got himself the 1919 rural New Brunswick version of grounded. In an attempt to impress the object of his affection and make a dashing exit from their evening of courting at her home, he urged the horse with family sleigh attached to a full gallop. As he attempted to round the gatepost at the end of her drive, the sleigh hit a bump and overturned. The horse escaped unscathed but the family sleigh was a shambles. My father suffered a broken nose, two black eyes and a large measure of indignity.

These days a teenager would have the car keys confiscated. My father received a similar punishment for the times. He was denied access to the horse, the *new* sleigh and, when spring finally rolled around, the buggy. As a result, he spent the next several months traveling to visit his lady fair on horseback, the Percheron's only trappings an old plaid blanket and a working-class bridle complete with draft horse blinders. Years later, after he'd had an opportunity to read Cervantes, he commented that he would have made Don Quixote look good.

Much as I loved these stories, it was the yarn he always recited on frosty Christmas afternoons that thrilled me most because it was participatory. Weather permitting, my father and I would don our skates at the millpond below my grandfather's house and head up the frozen brook into the forest. Only the swish-click of our skates, my snow-white ones keeping time with my father's long-bladed ones called reachers, broke the winter silence as we glided through the snowy landscape, dodging bits of bark and fallen branches lodged in the ice. The keen cold set my cheeks tingling as I stretched to keep pace.

When an early winter's twilight began to descend, we'd turn back toward home and my father would begin to recite *The Skater and the Wolves*, the tale of a lone skater pursued by a pack of wolves. As we glided along in the encroaching darkness, the poem took on life, and I slipped into the skates of the story's fleeing hero. My heartbeat quickened and my mittened hand clutched my father's gloved one just a little tighter as I glanced furtively into the shadows creeping out from among the trees.

Of course, the fictional character always made it to safety just as we arrived back at the millpond where a bon fire surrounded by family and friends kept the winter night's darkness at bay. As we skated into the dancing circle of light, a sense of satisfaction and security tinged with a sprinkling of sadness would engulf me. Another wonderful Christmas enriched by my father's stories was coming to an end.

I never tired of hearing his Yuletide yarns. They brightened the dark hours of a winter's solstice and were as much a tradition of the holiday seasons as fruit cake, turkey, and presents. As I pass them along to my children, I hope they'll appreciate and preserve these intangible gifts that were a precious part of my childhood Christmases.

Quarantined for Christmas

Sadly, some animosities don't vanish into the good will and fellowship that are supposed to characterize Christmas. My father found this out when he was a young lad and went a-courting one fine winter's day.

Family feuds have been around as long as there have been kinfolk. They've been fictional such as the bitterness between Shakespeare's Montagues and Capulets and deadly real such as the battle between the Hatfields and McCoys. Their causes have been as serious as murder and as ridiculous as a misunderstanding over a pig. Some have even been lost in the mists of time making the lingering alienation and bitterness meaningless as well as pointless.

Such was the case with the feud between my father's family and their three-farms-distant neighbors the MacDonalds. This source of yet another of my father's stories brings a Christmas chuckle to my heart.

Although there were suggestions the cause of animosity was ancient, having been carried from Scotland like a disease when the ancestors of both present-time families had immigrated to Canada, nothing was ever definitely proven. Suffice it to say, my father's family and the MacDonalds were sworn enemies based on tradition.

Therefore, when fifteen-year-old Iona Macdonald

caught my sixteen-year-old father's eye, it did not bode well. And when my father boldly used the family sleigh to drive Iona home from a quilting bee, one frosty evening early in December, long simmering, ill will escalated to a rolling boil.

In ringing tones, my grandfather forbade his son ever to see "that MacDonald girl" again. Furthermore, my father was denied the use of any of the farm horses for the rest of the winter. Granddad may have chosen this time period, believing (or at least hoping) their passion wouldn't outlast the season.

Unfortunately there were two other aspects of the teenage psyche that he didn't take into consideration. These, of course, were determination and defiance.

For three weeks my father obeyed the edict. Then hormones took over. On Christmas Eve afternoon he hitched a ride with a neighbor on the pretense of going to the church to help decorate for the evening service. As the sleigh drew abreast of the MacDonald farm, he jumped.

Five minutes later he intercepted the fair Iona as she emerged from the henhouse with a basket of eggs. Ten minutes later the resourceful lass had smuggled him into the house via the outdoor cellar hatch.

Over the next half hour, through a daring series of sock-footed sprints and stops, he made his way undetected up two flights of stairs, as Iona had directed, to the attic. There, with bated breath and pounding heart, he awaited the arrival of his true love.

The plan was that after a few blissful minutes of hand holding and chaste kisses, Iona would go back downstairs to dress for the Christmas Eve service. After the family had left for church, he'd steal out of the house and catch a ride with one of the families headed in the same direction as the MacDonalds.

Unfortunately the best laid plans...

Earlier that day Iona's younger sister Isobel had been feeling ill. While my father and Iona had been enjoying their stolen moments, the doctor had arrived, diagnosed Isobel as having contracted Scarlet Fever, and quarantined the house and its inhabitants for two weeks.

Informed of this appalling development when she returned downstairs, Iona took the first opportunity to scamper back to the attic and inform her beloved.

His first thought was to escape and head back to his father's farm but after Iona left him once more alone he realized that couldn't happen. He couldn't go home, possibly carrying an infectious disease to his family. He had to stay, make his presence known to Mr. and Mrs. MacDonald, and send a message to his parents that he was alive and, as of yet, well. He couldn't allow his mother to face Christmas worrying over the mysterious disappearance of her middle son.

With visions of walking for the rest of his life and shoveling mountain-high mounds of manure, he made his way down the attic stairs.

After the initial upheaval created by his appearance had died down, after Mr. MacDonald had called him a goodly number of unpleasant names, after he'd been assured that word of his whereabouts would be sent to his parents, my father settled down to serve his sentence.

Indeed, more of a sentence than he'd anticipated he discovered on the first morning of his stay. Roused from his hard cot in the kitchen a good two hours before daybreak, he was ordered to pull on his boots, coat, and cap and follow Mr. MacDonald out to feed the stock.

He didn't mind all that much. The same would have been expected of him at home. But when he returned to the kitchen, cold and ravenous for the likes of one of his mother's Christmas morning breakfasts of eggs, sausages, bacon, bread, and jam, he was appalled to find only a bowl of lumpy oatmeal and a cup of strong tea. While the MacDonalds tucked into the porridge, my father felt the first pangs of homesickness.

As the day progressed, he discovered the MacDonalds held to many of the traditions of Christmas in the Old Country. There was no Christmas tree and only a few of the most practical of presents such as hand knitted mittens and scarves. But worst of all, at noon, instead of the turkey, stuffing, gravy, cranberries, vegetables, and mincemeat pies he knew would grace his mother's table, there appeared on the MacDonald's board a true Scottish Christmas treat. When Mrs. MacDonald placed the great, gray mound he recognized as haggis in the centre of the table, his stomach roiled. And when boiled potatoes were passed around to be dipped in melted butter and oatmeal, he nearly gave in to tears.

In the days that followed, Mr. MacDonald, a canny Scot who'd been blessed with two daughters, decided to get as much work as possible out of the wayward youth. My father mucked out the cow barn, shoveled the pig sty, and cleaned the henhouse. He claimed he chopped enough wood to fuel the MacDonald stoves and fireplaces for the next two years and mended a harness so old it must have come from Scotland with Mr. MacDonald's grandfather.

As if this wasn't enough, Iona began to lose her appeal. He'd been a prisoner in her home for only two days when the true personality of his beloved started to reveal its unattractive self. While absence from Iona had indeed made his heart grow fonder…so fond he'd gotten himself into one of the worst scrapes in his life…he discovered that familiarity can indeed breed contempt.

During the early part of his captivity she'd been sweet and downright coquettish. Dressed in her Sunday best she'd cavorted about the kitchen that had become his home, tossing her golden curls and being every bit the beguiling creature who'd lured him into this entrapment.

But when her mother had advised her that Christmas was over and it was time to put away her finery and get back to work, quite another Iona appeared. She argued and whined until her scowling father appeared, and she stamped upstairs in tears to change her clothes.

She did her chores at a snail's pace, complaining loudly and making a poor job of whatever tasks her mother assigned to her. For a farm boy whose mother and sisters worked cheerfully from dawn to dusk, these were glaring shortcomings. In the evenings she sat scowling at the kitchen table while her mother wound rags into hair my love-smitten father had believed to be a natural tangle of beguiling waves and curls.

Worst of all were the meals. Bland, watery soups and stews regularly graced the MacDonald board. Vegetables either mush or so hard they had to be gnawed lay on his plate beside pieces of meat tougher than the old harness he had mended. Mrs. MacDonald's bread came from the oven baked as hard and dry as clay. He felt he'd retch if he saw another bit of salt herring on the supper table.

Iona, he discovered, like her mother, couldn't cook. Her biscuits could break windows and teeth; her cakes had the flavor and texture of sawdust. To a young man who enjoyed food and was accustomed to his mother's fine culinary skills, this was a major shortcoming.

My father knew he'd been wrong to sneak into the MacDonald house for a romantic tryst, and he deserved to be punished but surely this was overkill.

Finally the two weeks ended. Isobel, pale but recovered, was allowed to venture out of her room. And my father was permitted to return home.

Feeling like the prodigal son, he nevertheless walked the five miles home in record time. He wondered what punishment his father, a strict disciplinarian, would have in store. One thing he knew for certain. The family's fatted calf would be safe.

His stomach grumbled. *Please, please, please, just let me have one decent meal before I have to face the music.*

The heady smells of a roast beef dinner gushed out to greet him as he opened the kitchen door.

"Gordon!" His mother rushed to hug him. "Oh, it's good to have you home!"

My father looked over her shoulder at the platter of roast beef in the centre of the big oak table, at the steaming bowls of potatoes, carrots, and gravy, at the pie and rolls, then at his brothers and sisters seated around it and, finally, at his father at its head.

No one else spoke. The old clock on the shelf in the corner ticked. The fire in the big wood stove crackled. His stomach rumbled

"Sit down." Finally Granddad reached for the platter of meat and jerked his head in the direction of my father's usual chair. "And let this be the end of it. Anyone forced to eat Effie MacDonald's cooking for two weeks has suffered enough."

Christmas Mysteries

Last year I was delighted to discover that, even in the hustle and commercialism of a department store, I could find yet another inspiration that would help my heart once again find the magic of Christmas.

That stimulation was just inside the door of the establishment; wicker trays of candied fruit wrapped in cellophane decorated with big, red bows. Happy memories flooded back. A smile crinkled across my face as I carefully placed the nicest looking one in my cart. Finally I had one of my very own!

From my earliest recollections of Christmas, I'd been fascinated by candied fruit. Each year my grandmother's sister, my great aunt Molly, sent Nanna a tray of the confections from Boston. I waited for the delivery of the sturdy, cardboard box much more eagerly than my grandmother. She'd simply unwrap it, gaze at the fruit for a moment, then, with a sigh of "Oh, Molly," (I never learned the reason for this reaction) place it on the parlor mantel.

In my perception, each fruit tray was a thing of mysterious beauty. The bright red cherries, the golden pineapple, and the glistening dark dates and figs resplendent in their sugar coating beneath gleaming cellophane were items of infinite wonder.

The day finally arrived when the tray was unwrapped and presented for the enjoyment of

Christmas visitors. I was never offered any of the fruit, not even what was left after the visiting marauders had finished with it. It was, I presumed, considered a grown-up delicacy.

The slight didn't offend me. The impulse called curiosity regarding the fruit's taste did rear its head but I always managed to stifle it. I couldn't bear the thought of its flavor not living up to the ambrosia of my imagination. Better to keep the fantasy intact.

The sight of the remaining figs and odd pieces of pineapple laying helter-skelter in their woven basket—the cherries never lasted—seemed as sad a sight as when I found one of my snow tunnels crushed by neighborhood boys.

The arrival of the candied fruit tray marked the first of many magic mysteries of Christmas at my grandparents' house. Next there was the amazing phenomenon of how sugar would magically stick to the warm doughnuts Nanna had fried in the big cast iron pan on the wood stove.

Then there was the mystery of the missing chickens. Every year, mid December, two of my grandfather's Rhode Island Reds disappeared. Granddaddy said they'd wandered off and had probably found another family to live with. It was years before I connected the two golden brown birds my grandmother served up for Christmas dinner with those hens that had regularly disappeared.

I was about the same age, five or six, when I realized that the reason the plum pudding my grandmother steamed in the oven days before the big event magically burst into flames when touched with a match was because of its dousing with the contents of the bottle she kept tucked in the back of the kitchen cupboard. Brandy was not a word I was yet familiar with.

An even bigger mystery was how Santa got down the chimney. The big fireplace between the parlor and dining room was never lit on Christmas Eve so the hearty old fellow was in no danger of being turned into a ball of flame on entry. Still, looking up the flue, I couldn't imagine how he managed to get down its not-so-wide length.

My grandfather explained that Santa was a spirit and, therefore, could make himself into any size necessary to visit good children. Nevertheless, each Christmas Eve, I found myself on my hands and knees peering up into the blackness…not entirely convinced Granddaddy had it right.

What Granddaddy did have a firm handle on was a direct line to Santa. I'll never forget the Christmas he arranged to have the Jolly Old Elf alter his schedule to pay me an early evening visit.

I must have been misbehaving one Christmas Eve afternoon when he suggested Santa might drop in after supper to see what I was up to.

Slightly apprehensive, I settled down to eat my supper. Shortly after the meal, when Granddaddy had gone out to feed the chickens, I heard it. My heart leaped and seemed to stop.

Sleigh bells and definitely prancing and pawing on the verandah roof!

It took every ounce of my willpower not to rush out into the yard and look up, Granddaddy's admonitions of years previous echoing across my mind. If I ever tried to actually see Santa, he'd told me one Christmas Eve when I'd been especially slow in going to bed, my "nice" rating would plummet into the naughty range. Every child with the least bit of Santa knowledge knew what that meant.

So I sat at the kitchen table, hands clasped so tightly my knuckles turned as white as the dooryard snow. My breath clogged in my throat as I listened to the magic of the moment.

A scuffling noise suggested lift-off. Then all was quiet, except for the ticking of the kitchen clock.

My breathing was just beginning to return to normal when Granddaddy returned. He stamped snow from his boots and began to unbutton his mackinaw.

"Granddaddy, he was here!" I leaped up to seize his cold hand. "I heard him…up on the roof! We have to go out and look for tracks!"

"I thought I saw something in the sky when I came out of the chicken coop," he said thoughtfully. "So he did make it. I must remember to thank him."

"Come on, come on!" I tugged at his hand. "I want to see where he landed."

As I stood in the dooryard moments later, Granddaddy placed a ladder against the edge of the roof, and climbed up to inspect the freshly fallen snow.

"What do you see? What do you see?" I jumped up and down. "Are there hoof prints? Can you see if Santa walked around up there?"

By now, Granddaddy had reached the verandah roof and bent to examine the snow.

"Yes, yes," he said. "There are hoof prints…a lot of them. Some kind of deer, I'd say. And a few boot marks, too."

"Let me see, let me see!" I cried starting up the ladder.

"No, no." Granddaddy was already on the top rung and beginning to descent. "It's slippery up here. Your grandmother wouldn't allow you on the roof. And I don't think Santa would be happy to know you were checking up on *him*."

His last sentence stopped me with one foot on the first rung. Hoping I'd already passed the naughty-nice test on the positive side, I wasn't about to risk losing my rating.

That was a long time ago. Coming back to the moment, I went down a few more store aisles with their festive frippery and piped-in holiday hits, those memories warming my heart. I headed back to the fruit display at the front of the store, carefully replaced that lovely tray on the shelf, and pushed my cart toward the check-out.

I wanted to leave one Christmas mystery intact.

A Christmas Call

"Almost seven thirty." My grandfather pulled his gold watch from his vest pocket and held it out as far as it would reach on its fob to squint at the time. "We should be getting ready to go over."

By "over" he meant to my parents' house across the backyard. The two houses shared a telephone located there. Since it was Christmas Eve the entire family would congregate around it and wait for that much anticipated ring that meant my uncle who lived in Alberta was on the line.

In the 1950's long distance calls were expensive, to be used only in emergencies or on very special occasions such as this, the Yuletide call from western Canada to our home on the east coast. My uncle Loris came home every second July and wrote weekly but the Christmas call was something to be anticipated with excitement and joy.

Glancing at my grandparents as they donned their coats, hats, and boots, I recognized the expressions on their faces. I'd once glimpsed myself in the hall mirror late one Christmas Eve when Santa's visit was imminent.

"Put on your coat, darlin'." My grandfather's words always echoed his Celtic roots when he was happy. "The yard is slippery. We don't want to be late."

"Yes, Granddaddy." I glanced wishfully at the heap

of presents on the oil-cloth-covered kitchen table. I'd eaten supper at my grandparents' house to participate in piling them there after the meal was cleared away. A family Yuletide tradition, gift opening took place in their kitchen after receiving my uncle's call. It was much warmer near the oil stove than in the parlor where the decorated Christmas tree stood well preserved in the chill of the unheated room. With a final look and a sigh, I struggled into my coat and boots. Christmas Eve was not a time to be belligerent.

We started across the short distance that separated our houses, my grandmother on my grandfather's arm. Brimming with seven-year-old Christmas excitement, I slid and skidded ahead on the ice. Soon we'd get the call and could move on to gift opening. Later, much later, after I'd been bundled off to bed, there'd be the visit from the Jolly Old Elf.

I'm not saying I didn't enjoy Uncle Loris's call. He had a ranch near Smokey Lake with horses and dogs, the two creatures I fancied with all my heart and soul. But he didn't talk about them much, mostly wanted to know about us and how we were. Anyhow, I couldn't pet them over a telephone wire.

I looked up at the stars, diamonds in a sea of black velvet, and sucked in a breath of cold, clear air. I spread my arms wide and swung around and around in an effort to view all of them.

"Granddaddy, are those the same stars that were shining on the night Jesus was born?" I asked.

"Exact same ones, darlin'."

"And was one of them the one that the shepherds and wise men followed to…?"

"Come along, Gail." My grandmother, never as

patient with my meanderings and musings as my grandfather, spoke sharply.

"Coming, Nanna." I slid the rest of the way and bumped to a halt at the bottom of the steps.

"Always dreaming, that child." Nanna shook her head and proceeded inside as my grandfather held the door open for her and me. Granddaddy winked as I passed him.

"One of them was," he bent to whisper into my ear. "Maybe that real bright one right over your Dad's roof."

Inside my parents greeted Nanna and Granddaddy before we all made our way into the dining room where the *phone* sat on a small table in the corner. Chairs had been placed around it in a semi-circle, and we settled down to wait.

"The yard is very icy." My mother made an attempt at small talk even though the air fairly crackled with anticipation.

"Ice, ice, and more ice," Nanna replied adjusting herself into a comfortable position. "We never had winters like this when I was a child."

"Makes for good skating on the river though." Granddaddy nudged me and slanted a conspiratorial look.

"Sure does." My father joined in. "I remember one Christmas when I was eight or ten and all I wanted was screws to fasten blades to a pair of old boots so that I could skate on the mill pond."

"I've asked for skates this year…" My comment was interrupted by the *phone*. Its ring made us all start. Even though it was expected, our nerves were on edge.

My father, as always, was the designated one to answer.

"Hello. Loris?" He spoke louder than normal; reception was never good. "Merry Christmas. Yes, we're all here. How is the weather in Alberta? Good, good. Here, I'll let you speak to your mother."

My grandmother, her eyes shining like the stars in the Christmas sky, took the receiver carefully, gingerly, as if she were afraid she might sever the connection. "Loris, hello, dear."

Her conversation lasted only a few minutes before, with tears in her eyes, she bade her son farewell until July and handed the receiver to my grandfather.

"Merry Christmas, son. How's everything? Livestock doing well? Do you have much snow? That cold, eh? How are Isabelle and the boy? Yes, yes, we'll take a turn talking to them."

My mother spoke next, and then the phone was handed to me to speak to my cousin Bobby. The adults always seemed to think children wanted to speak to children when what I really wanted to do was talk to my gregarious aunt who would tell me about their horses and dogs.

Finally my father took the phone to wind up the call, and it was over for another year. As he replaced the receiver on the cradle, Nanna pulled a handkerchief from the sleeve of her sweater and sniffed into it. Granddaddy cleared his throat.

"Well," he said. "Well."

I waited patiently. There were always a few moments of silence after the call. Then my father stood and winked at me. "Maybe we should head back across the yard. I'd say it's just about time to open presents."

"Yes." Granddaddy pulled out his watch and cleared his throat again. "I'd say it's just about that time."

We bundled into coats, hats, and boots for the short pilgrimage across the yard. This time I didn't pause to star gaze. Eagerness sent me gliding over the ice.

"Be careful, child!" Nanna's admonition slowed me down just a tad.

I got my skates that Christmas. My father and I went gliding across the mill pond the next day. His skates, long bladed contraptions called reachers, a present from my mother, were new, too. His days of asking for screws to fashion a pair from old boots were behind him.

These days stories about skate screws and the magic of a Christmas call have become familial anecdotes. Communications have undergone such immense changes since those times of the Christmas call that my parents and grandparents would have believed them to be the stuff of science fiction.

This Yuletide, as I sit at my computer and receive e-mails from family and friends, knowing that Skype and such marvels as web cams and Instant Messenger are also available, I marvel at how far we've come in the field of communications. At the click of a mouse, I can be connected with people around the world and get not only verbal but also visual images of their lives. I wonder what Nanna would have thought of these marvelous creations. I know Granddaddy would have been thrilled.

I look out a window and gaze up at the stars, at one particularly bright one, and remember him. Him and his tolerance for my meanderings. And know that the true marvels of the Christmas season haven't really changed at all.

The Cedar Chest's Secret

For many years, I've kept my guilt regarding the cedar chest a secret, ashamed of my lack of self-control. This Christmas I've decided to make a clean breast of it and confess.

To begin with, I admit to being an incurable bookaholic. I always have been. One of my earliest memories is of standing behind my mother as she washed the lunch dishes, pulling at her apron strings as I begged her to read "just one more chapter, please, just one more chapter."

I don't recall my mother ever refusing to leave the sudsy pan, dry her hands, and follow me to the living room. We'd curl up together and while away the afternoon, deep in our love for the printed word. A devoted amateur actress, she read with passionate expression. I would listen, mesmerized, carried away on the wings of her words.

When I finally learned to read on my own, I experienced one of the greatest epiphanies of my life. There was magic to be found on the printed page; words had the power to sweep me into another time, another place, another spirit.

I read everything from the cereal box on the breakfast table to the set of university encyclopedias published in 1902 which I discovered in my grandmother's attic. (It wasn't until I couldn't find the word "airplane" that I recognized the venerable age of this fascinating reading material and stopped using then as reference material for school projects).

I soon wanted my own library. While other children hounded their parents for toys, I begged for books, books, and more books.

Christmas presented a paramount opportunity for my supplications. Each autumn I prepared a long list of titles, any of which I'd be delighted to find beneath the tree. Since we had no bookstore in our small town, Eaton's catalogue was the only source of these desirable items.

One very special Sunday afternoon each November, my mother and I would sit at the kitchen table, that lovely plump volume open in front of us, while I selected the books I most desired from the limited selection on the pair of pages offering reading material.

My mother, wise to my penchant for devouring books the moment they arrived in the house, never let me know when she was picking up the parcel from the post office. She most definitely never revealed where she hid the package until Christmas.

By this time, my addiction to books had made me sly and unscrupulous. No book could remain unread anywhere within my ability to ferret it out. One day when I'd become desperate for a good, fresh read, I began a quest for her hiding place.

I dug through closets, into their darkest, most remote corners and topmost shelves. I burrowed under the sheets and towels in the linen cupboard, and even checked beneath the mattress in the guest room.

Stymied, later that afternoon I followed my mother into my parent's bedroom and sat down on the edge of the bed. I watched as she opened the cedar chest beneath the window. My father had made it for her when they'd gotten engaged, and she kept her most treasured possessions inside…her wedding gown, my christening dress, her collection of hand-embroidered linens and, anathemas to a fan of children's writer Thornton W. Burgess, her fox fur capes. The wily hero of many of Mr. Burgess's stories, Reddy Fox had found his way into my heart and left me with an abhorrence of all garments made from animal pelts. My mother, well aware of the fact, must have believed that nothing could induce me to invade the cedar chest that housed them.

I watched as she folded a pillowslip she'd finished decorating with moss roses. As she bent over the cedar chest to store her handiwork, I started to turn away.

Something caught my eye. Peeking out from beneath a lace tablecloth was the top corner of a shiny new book!

Possibly realizing her *faux pas*, my mother hastily lowered the lid and glanced in my direction. Had I seen it? The question mirrored in her eyes.

Struggling to appear nonchalant, I began to hum, "We Wish You a Merry Christmas" as I swung my legs against the chenille bedspread and gazed up at the ceiling. She hesitated, then drew a deep breath, and headed out of the room.

"Come along, Gail," she called as she started down the stairs. "We have cookies to bake."

I skipped along after her, visions of how I'd invade the cedar chest later when I was alone upstairs dancing through my head.

That evening, after I'd been tucked into bed and my parents were settled in the living room listening to

Charlie McCarthy and Edgar Bergen on the radio, I slipped my bare feet out onto the cold linoleum and tiptoed across the hall to my parents' room. I carried a small flashlight my father had given me the previous Christmas...in case of power outages, he'd said. I'm sure he'd never intended it to be used for book burglary in his own home.

Trembling with the thrill of the forbidden, I eased open the cedar chest, slipped my hand beneath the folded linens, holding my breath and grimacing as my hand brushed against the furs of those poor, dead foxes, and felt them...not the usual two but four, count them, *four* slick, new books, their dust jackets smooth and beautiful as silk.

I slid out the top volume and read its title, *The Secret of Shadow Ranch.* It was the Nancy Drew mystery I'd craved for the past two years, but Eatons had always sent a substitution. My breath caught in my throat.

Resting my back against the cedar chest, I sat on the floor, opened the Carolyn Keene classic to page one, adjusted my flashlight, and began to read. I had to stay alert for the slightest indication that either of my parents was about to come upstairs.

Oh, the bliss of those stolen moments. My heart hammering, I read Nancy's adventures for more than an hour. My feet felt like blocks of ice on the cold floor, I shivered in my pajamas...and I continued to read.

Then I heard my father suggesting a cup of tea before bed. I eased open the cedar chest, slid the book gently back beneath the tablecloths, and scuttled back to my room.

Snuggled beneath the covers with the flashlight still

warm in my hand, I drifted off to sleep. Visions of Nancy Drew and her friends Bess and George riding the range at Shadow Ranch replaced the sugarplums that were supposed to dance through my head.

The next morning, as I glanced across the breakfast at my mother, guilt washed over me. I was destroying her joy in the big surprise she must be planning to spring on me on Christmas morning with the presentation of that long-desired Nancy Drew title.

I tried to admonish myself. *You should be ashamed of yourself. You must never, never do it again.*

Yet that night, as my parents listened to a Christmas concert on the living room radio, I once again eased open the pages of *The Secret of Shadow Ranch* and read on. By the time Christmas Eve arrived, I'd devoured all four books and was contemplating rereading *Shadow Ranch*.

No, I told myself sternly. *You'll bend a page, you'll crack the spine. You'll leave evidence. Quit while you're ahead.*

As I unwrapped each book on Christmas morning, my gushing enthusiasm might have been a tip-off to less trusting parents. Both avid readers, they understood (or believed they understood) the extent of my thirst for the printed word. My mother, confident in the fact that nothing could induce me to touch those fox furs much less burrow beneath them, watched me, her expression bright in my reflected joy. Cradling my treasures in my arms, I curled up in a corner of the couch and, in the glow of the multi-colored tree lights, settled down to indulge myself in a full Christmas morning of reading.

My clandestine activity continued during the next three Christmases. It might have gone on longer had I not made a major mistake.

My favorite author at the time was L. M. Montgomery. I'd read all of the Anne books and had been longing for one of the author's more mature stories called *The Blue Castle* Not an easy book to find, it was proving as elusive as *The Secret of Shadow Ranch* years earlier.

But joy of joys! A week before Christmas it appeared in the cedar chest. Reading it by the light of my flashlight, I was thrilled by the courage of heroine, Valancy Stirling, and identified with her desire for freedom and self-expression. It was so romantic, the ending so absolutely wonderful. When I finished it two days before Christmas, I hugged the volume in the darkness beside the cedar chest. Perfect, perfect little book!

On Christmas morning relatives descended on our home. It was my parents' turn to host the Yuletide dinner. One of my maternal aunts wandered into the living room to find me in my usual corner of the couch, rereading *The Blue Castle*.

"Well, Gail, I see you got another book," she sighed in mild exasperation.

"Yes, a perfectly lovely book." I put my finger between the pages of the first chapter to mark my place and beamed at her.

"Another novel, no doubt," she scoffed, sitting down opposite me. "I never read anything but the newspapers myself. Those things are nothing but nonsense."

"Oh, no they aren't!" I couldn't bear to hear my beloved books defamed. "This one is about a girl who leaves home to nurse a sick friend and falls in love with the town outcast. Later she discovers he's really a millionaire, they get married, and live happily ever after."

"Do they now?"

My stomach doing a flip flop, I turned to see my mother standing in the living room doorway. My finger slipped from page six.

Her lips curled into a smile. She winked and turned back into the turkey-scented kitchen.

My mother died several Christmases later, a victim of cancer. Her legacy to my love of literature lives on in my heart and home. *The Adventures of Reddy Fox*, *The Secret of Shadow Ranch*, and *The Blue Castle* remain beloved parts of my library. As for the cedar chest, it sits in my living room, symbolic of those happy Christmases when a book and a mother who understood could make my dreams come true.

A Scholar and a Gentleman

It may have been my father's story telling that first aroused my desire to become a writer but one Christmas, a Christmas I will never forget, it was my mother's kindness that inadvertently gave my ambition a benchmark push in the right direction.

Christmas would fall on Friday that year. Relief flooded through my eight-year-old veins as I perused the month of December on the kitchen calendar. That meant Uncle Johnny wouldn't be at our house for either Christmas Eve supper or dinner the following day.

I resented Uncle Johnny. His presence at our supper table every Wednesday evening never failed to spoil my enjoyment of the meal.

Uncle Johnny was eighty-six. He had watery, red-rimmed eyes, sagging jowls, and trembling hands that slopped and spilled food and drink. Sometimes drool seeped from the corners of his mouth *and* he smelled of moth balls.

He always arrived wearing an old-fashioned, shiny-with-age, three-piece suit, snow-white shirt, a threadbare tie bearing some sort of insignia, and down-at-the heels black shoes glossed to a military shine. A polished fob crossing his vest terminated in the breast pocket that held his gold watch.

I blamed my mother for Uncle Johnny's visits. At her insistence, my father, on his way home from work each Wednesday evening, would pick up Uncle Johnny. And he wasn't even her uncle. He was just a second cousin of my grandfather's who'd ended up alone in old age. Nevertheless, welcoming this type of family connection into our home was typical of my mother. Later in life, when I read the words in the Book of Ruth, "Your people shall be my people" I realized my mother had lived that philosophy. My father's family had become hers on the day they'd married and would remain as such for her all of her life.

Uncle Johnny lived in a once-genteel, now shabby boarding house beside the town's newspaper office. His proximity to this print shop facilitated the neatly bound type-set copies of his poems and essays he never failed to bring as gifts to my mother.

He'd present one of the four inch by four inch pale blue binders to her each Wednesday just as we sat down to supper. My mother's meal would grow cold on her plate as she read. Uncle Johnny, with shaking hands, dribbled food down the napkin he'd tucked under his chin as he cast not-so-furtive glances in her direction awaiting her reaction.

Repulsed, I tried to keep my eyes focused on the meal in front of me and ignore Uncle Johnny's effort to get food and drink to his mouth.

My mother would finish reading, clutch the small binder to her chest, and smile.

"Lovely, Uncle Johnny, absolutely lovely," she'd breathe. "I'll treasure it."

He'd cast her an adoring, watery smile as he patted his mouth with a corner of his napkin.

"Thank you, my dear," he'd reply softly, giving a gentle nod of appreciative acknowledgement in her direction. "You're too kind."

On Wednesday of Christmas week that year, aglow with hope and plans for the Yuletide, I was willing to view even Uncle Johnny's weekly dinner visit in a kinder light. He wouldn't be around to spoil any of the Christmas feasts.

That morning my mother shattered my anticipation.

"I've invited Uncle Johnny to come on Friday," I overheard her telling my father. "Last week when I asked about his plans for Christmas, I discovered he hadn't any. Oh, he tried to say Cousin George had mentioned something back in the summer but I have a feeling he was fibbing. He didn't want us to invite him out of pity. I said that since there'd be just the three of us this year, he'd be doing us a favor by helping us to eat that big turkey you bought."

"No!" Startling my parents, I burst into the kitchen. "No! No! No! He'll spoil everything with his shaking and drooling and dribbling! And he smells!"

"Gail, how can you say such dreadful things!" My mother's expression exuded her hurt and dismay. "Uncle Johnny is a dear, old gentleman. He's kind and clever and…"

"I hate him, I hate him!" I yelled. "If he's here for Christmas, I won't come to the table!"

I stormed up to my room and slammed the door.

A half hour later (my allowed cooling off time) my father entered. I knew from his expression I was in deep trouble.

"You've hurt your mother's feelings," he said, his face grim. "I want you to apologize to her." He turned to leave, then paused.

"And if you refuse to share Christmas dinner with

Uncle Johnny, Santa definitely won't be pleased."

Consequently Christmas Day saw me seated in my usual place across from Uncle Johnny. As my mother placed the steaming, golden brown turkey on the table, he drew a small, awkwardly wrapped package from inside his suit coat. With a shaking hand he extended it toward me.

"Your mother tells me you enjoy reading and hope to be a writer some day," he said, his thin, old voice quavering. "I thought you might enjoy this."

I stared down at the crumpled wrappings. Some tatty old thing not even wrapped in new paper.

"Open it, Gail." My mother beamed down on both of us.

Gingerly I untied the wrinkled ribbon and spread wide the paper. Inside was a book, *Emily of New Moon* by L.M. Montgomery.

"It's about a young lady about your age who, much like you, loves animals and aspires to be a writer," Uncle Johnny explained, a tremulous smile on his moist lips.

"How thoughtful, Uncle Johnny." My mother put an arm around the shoulders of his worn jacket and hugged him. "Gail, wasn't that thoughtful of Uncle Johnny?"

"Yes." I was turning the book slowly over in my hands. Used. I liked fresh, new books. But Uncle Johnny had said it was about a girl who loved animals and wanted to write... "Thank you, Uncle Johnny."

"You're most welcome, my dear. I hope it will inspire you."

He handed my mother a parcel he'd placed on the corner of the table before sitting down. It was double the size of his usual blue binder offerings and much thicker.

"For you," he said. "And Gordon." He glanced at my father.

My mother unwrapped it carefully. Inside lay a black three-ringed binder, the type you could purchase at any stationery store. For a moment she stared down at it, smiling but with a couple of quizzical wrinkles furrowing her forehead.

"Open it," Uncle Johnny urged, his sagging eyes bright. "I...I hope you like it. It's my magnum opus."

I heard her breath catch and saw her eyes widen as she stared at the first page.

"*The Fowlie Family History from 1500 to the Present*," she read aloud its title, then looked up at Uncle Johnny, her eyes glowing. "Oh, Uncle Johnny, how wonderful! Is this what you've been working on for so many years? Gordon, just look! What an absolute treasure!"

"Thank you, my dear, thank you." Uncle Johnny, shy under her billowing praise, drew his watch from his breast pocket and peered down at it. "Now perhaps we'd best set upon this lovely dinner you've prepared before it becomes cold."

Uncle Johnny passed away that spring, alone in his room at the boarding house. Few people attended his funeral. In his poverty and isolation, he'd been largely forgotten.

I stood by his grave clutching my mother's hand and *Emily of New Moon,* the book I'd come to cherish and whose author would have a major influence on my literary life.

"He spent his life working as an accountant for an insurance company," my mother told me. "Yet he'd graduated from one of the most prestigious universities in this country with the highest honors. Remember the insignia on that old tie he always wore? Sadly a degree in history and philosophy doesn't bode well for employment so there he sat year after year, making a living, his keen, creative mind moldering away in a stack of business ledgers when he longed to do historical research and write poetry. It was only in his final years…" Her voice broke, and she looked down at me, tears swimming in her eyes. "But he was always, always, a scholar and a gentleman."

In later years that family history Uncle Johnny had so painstakingly compiled, then tediously typed using multiple sheets of carbon paper, would become the basis of a number of my most successful stories. But perhaps, most important were the words I discovered tucked away on its back page, the warmth of the true Christmas spirit in each line.

"As I walk through the quiet beauty of Chatham's tree-lined streets, I meet Opal and her lovely little daughter, Gail. What a joy it is, as always, to see them both."

My Second Kingdom

That Christmas marked the beginning of a new and forever phase of my life. After reading Uncle Johnny's Christmas gift, I recognized what I would call my Second Kingdom, my world of writing.

It had been lurking somewhere in the recesses of my mind for years, since I'd first uncovered the magic to be found in books. Now, with *Emily of New Moon* as my guiding light, I felt vindicated in plunging ahead with the story ideas that had been simmering in my brain. The moment a "just right" idea hit, I now recognized it much as Emily welcomed and reveled in her "flashes."

Like fireworks and lightning, my creative world would explode with a starburst of light, sound, sensation, and color that put the opening of a Disney movie to shame. The drawbridge of my Second Kingdom would lower to let action and adventure, heroes and heroines, mystery and mayhem tumble helter-skelter over my imagination. My heart raced, my pulses soared. I'd wave my magic pencil, ready to create beauty and joy and suspense and drama and excitement all out of thin air.

On the wings of imagination, I'd fly away, leaving the dull, the boring, the pedantic far behind. I no longer heard the neighbor's incessantly barking Chihuahua or the radio in the living room. I'd left my home and body for the mystical realm called THE STORY.

Suspended in time and space, I'd enter the bodies and souls of my characters and set them free. I'd see, taste, touch, smell, and hear what they did, rise and fall with their victories and defeats, ache with their pain, laugh with their joy, sob with their sorrows. As the plot twisted and turned, I'd be astonished, astounded, horrified, saddened, amused, and, most of all, amazed at how these shadow people would act and react within its caldron. They'd grabbed the story line in their teeth and were off at an exhilarating gallop.

Enthralling figments of my imagination, they took control. Strengths and weaknesses shaping their lives and deeds, they moved through incident after incident, chapter after chapter until, finally, they reached that physical and psychological precipice…the climax.

They struggled, lives and souls in jeopardy. I felt their adrenaline rush, their hearts pounding. Then, with surging spirits, *we* triumphed!

As we slid, satisfied and grateful, into what I'd later learn to term the denouement, I'd breathe a contented sigh. The vision was fading but I couldn't feel sad or disappointed. I knew another would shortly come again in a starburst of light and sound and sensation.

In later years, my imaginings would next be off to an editor. Over the years, I've learned to handle acceptance and rejection without letting either overwhelm me. I've also learned that a story spurned in one market place can be touted in another. To lose faith in what I've created out of thin air after a first, fifth, or even fifteenth try would be to do it a grave injustice.

Fortunately, in a number of cases, there's been the acceptance letter, confirmation that the people and events I've brought into this world will have a future in the minds and imaginations of those wonderful beings called readers.

Of course, there's always a bit of a let-down that space between acceptance and publication, the writer's equivalent of the Baby Blues. Briefly, I'm back in the world of barking dogs, and blaring music.

But there's a simple cure. It's easy, it's magic. I scttle in front of my computer, flex my fingers, and once again head back to my Second Kingdom.

Thank you, Mom and Uncle Johnny, for that very special Christmas.

Do This in Remembrance of Me

Growing up, I was blessed with a large, extended family. My parents and I lived next door to my maternal grandparents and two wonderful aunts. I especially remember my Aunt Marion and her joy in the Christmas season. When she passed away, I inherited a number of her possessions, among them her beloved little, ceramic Christmas tree.

Each Yuletide I place the little ornament on the mantel in our living room, plug it in to an outlet, and find joy in its multicolored lights. Each time, I'm reminded of the words of the Communion service taken from the gospel of St. Matthew, Chapter 26, verses 20 through 29.

"Do this in remembrance of me," Jesus said.

It's in that spirit I place the little twelve-inch tree above the fireplace in memory of my Aunt Marion who loved the Christmas season so dearly. I do it in remembrance of her and the many acts of love and altruism that she performed each December.

Aunt Marion never married and lived for her first sixty years with her parents and sister in a big, old Victorian home in the centre of town. Blessed with a broad, bright smile she captured the hearts of everyone she met in her aura of optimism and friendliness. Most of all, she loved sharing and giving. Christmas offered her the perfect opportunity to do both.

Each December 25th when I was a child, after I'd had a couple of hours to enthuse over what Santa had left for me, Aunt Marion would arrive with a pillow case full of presents she said the Jolly Old Elf had mistakenly delivered to her house. The contents held all the mystery and magic of an unexpected treasure trove. It seemed that while Santa brought the gifts I'd requested to my house, he continually misdirected delights beyond my expectations to Aunt Marion's. The joy I experienced rummaging through that pillow slip returns each Christmas as I plug in that little ceramic tree.

In later years, Aunt Marion found herself alone and lonely in the rambling family home. Her parents and sister had passed away and with them the big family Christmas dinners that had been a tradition in their dining room. The children like myself for whom she'd helped Santa deliver gifts had grown up and moved away. She fell into a deep depression that doctors and psychiatrists were unable to alleviate or, I believe, fully appreciate.

Two weeks after Christmas the year she celebrated her seventy-second birthday she was diagnosed with brain cancer.

As I sat by her hospital bed where she lay unconscious after a devastating surgery, I recalled her glowing smile, her never-failing joy in the Yuletide season, and her many kindnesses not only to myself but to so many others. She'd lived a beautiful life through her joy of giving. When she passed away two weeks later, I was not alone in my heartbreak.

At her funeral three days later, the minister surprised the congregation by rising and, before speaking to them, looking heaven-ward.

"Marion, forgive me." His words startled us. "Forgive me for breaking my promise to you, but I've searched my heart and decided I must do as my conscience dictates." He turned back to the standing-room-only gathering.

"You all know Marion was a loving and giving person," he said. "You also know that these last few years she's felt an emptiness in her life, especially during the Christmas season. But still, she wanted to share. Toward this goal, she came to me and asked me if I knew of any families who were finding the Yuletide season financially difficult. Of course I did. So she wrote checks, generous checks made out to me that she might provide for them. She became their anonymous angel.

"Near the end, cancer robbed her of the ability to enjoy life but I believe, I must believe, that memories of all those good and wonderful Christmases, Christmases that she was responsible for making merry and bright lingered somewhere in her mind and gave her the sense of peace and contentment that only a life well lived can produce."

He looked up again and smiled. "I'm not concerned that you won't forgive me, Marion. Your generous heart will allow you to do no less."

Therefore, each year as I set up the little ceramic Christmas tree that she lighted with such joy every December 24th, I softly whisper my own version of those beautiful words of the Communion service: this I do in remembrance of you.

Her memory kindles the true meaning of Christmas in my heart.

Those Christmas Cranberries

While many of the memories of Christmas that light joy in my heart are warm and reverent like the story of Aunt Marion, others like the tale of my father's quarantine bring a chuckle. My recollection of how we got our Christmas cranberries one year is another such a story.

Cranberries have always been an integral part of our family Christmas dinner. Succulent and sweetly tart, they brighten our festive table and enhance the flavor of roast turkey. Nevertheless there was one year when I believe the memory of their acquisition soured my father's normal enjoyment of the crimson fruit and must have rendered them much more bitter than sweet.

It began one October morning about nine weeks before Christmas. My father and I had arrived at the marsh to do some duck hunting just as day was breaking. Unfortunately, it promised to be of the bluebird variety, full of clear skies and slack breezes, miserable conditions for duck hunting. Nevertheless, we sloshed through yards of sucking mud to put out our decoys, then struggled back to our blind to wait.

When three hours of patience yielded nothing but increasing sunshine and a few flocks passing so high overhead as to be little more than fly specks in the troposphere, my father grew restless.

"Nothing's going to come in today," he said

dropping his shells back into his jacket pocket and leaning his gun against our ambush. "Still, there's no need to go home empty-handed. When we were putting out the decoys, I saw some cranberries. We may as well pick them. Never too early to start planning for Christmas dinner."

Once again we struggled through the ooze until we'd reached the berries. The plumpest ones appeared to be farther out and so we slogged doggedly onward.

Glancing back at one point, I realized we'd passed our decoys. Now they floated serenely midway between us and the blind. For a moment the situation gave me pause. Then I shrugged. What did it matter? Nothing was going to come in that day. Putting the thought aside, I returned to filling my game bag with berries.

Around noon I glanced up to see yet another flock of high flying black ducks passing overhead. Apparently intent on some destination further along the bay, they, like all their predecessors, appeared ready to bypass our lures. Assuming this would be as close as I'd get to game that day, I straightened up and shielded my eyes to watch them strung out across the faultless blue.

The next instant my assumptions were shattered. One of their number had spotted our decoys. Undeterred by the two camouflage-garbed figures nearby, he whirled and began an easy downward glide to join the wooden impostures. His friends followed. Shortly twenty-five big black ducks had landed around our drawing cards not more than twenty yards from where my father and I stood ankle-deep in bog.

Slowly my father straightened from his berry picking. His mouth dropped open. His last handful plopped one by one into the thick black slime imprisoning his feet. An atheist confronted by a miracle could not have looked more astounded.

Careless of his condition, the ducks relaxed and, clucking like contented hens, began swimming placidly among our decoys. Eventually they swam so close to us I'm sure we could have killed a few if we'd had stones instead of cranberries at our disposal.

My father at that point, I figured, was seeing plenty of red without the help of any ruddy swamp fruit. Not a man easily driven to profanity, he suddenly burst into a description of those tantalizing birds which would have challenged the repertoire of a drunken sailor.

The birds, unimpressed, continued to swim in leisurely circles in and out among our decoys. Instinct seemed to be telling them they were as safe as a duck could possibly be. But, then, no one has ever successfully deciphered the deductions of a duck.

Finally my father could stand it no more. With a mighty roar, he reached into his game bag, grabbed a handful of cranberries, and flung them at those irritating birds.

"Get!" he yelled.

Squawking their annoyance, the flock rose up into the blue and was soon out of sight.

After they'd gone, we made our way to shore. We didn't speak. No words were adequate in such a situation.

Only when we reached our blind to find a freshly dead black duck at the base of a tree behind it did my father's power of speech return.

"Must have flown into that white birch and broken its neck," he muttered staring down at it. "Probably happened while he was looking back over his shoulder, laughing at us!"

From his expression when he tasted the cranberries that Christmas, I guessed that all the sugar in Cuba couldn't completely erase the bitterness of the memory that Yuletide condiment inspired.

The Christmas of the China Dog

Christmases have a way of becoming monikered. For example, I recall The Christmas Aunt Molly Visited and The Christmas Janet Got Engaged. For me the most outstanding was the one I named The Christmas of the China Dog.

Twelve years old at the time, I had a passion that held me in its grasp. For all of the dozen years that constituted my life to that date I'd been a passionate dog fancier. From my earliest recollections, I remembered being enamored with canines. One of my favorite baby photos shows me beside a big, white, stuffed dog. He's in a chair, I'm standing beside him. That pose speaks volumes about my regard for Fluffy.

As I came of age to be allowed to play outside alone, I'd stand at the gate and wait for a dog, any dog, to pass by. Then I'd try to lure him into the yard to play.

When I'd asked, begged, and pleaded for a dog of my own, my parents simply replied that I was too young for the responsibility. But this year I'd reached the age of baby-sitting maturity. Surely someone who could be trusted alone with young children could be judged capable of caring for one small, chewing, piddling puppy.

I had good reason to hope that December. All the signs were there. My parents, being especially secretive, definitely were conspiring something big and exciting.

Oh, sure, there was only one small, mysterious box for me under the tree (the rest with my name on them readily identifiable as books and clothing) but that, I deduced in my fanciful mind, contained a collar and leash. On Christmas morning my Collie puppy would be brought into the living room, a big red bow around his neck. I'd immediately name him Prince, and he and I would never again be separated...except for the demands of church and school.

I didn't think I would survive the final seven days prior to Christmas. Plans for my dog overwhelmed my every waking minute and dreams of my precious pooch filled my nights.

I tingled, I hugged myself, I burst into song at odd and, often for those around me, startling moments. Although I occasionally caught my parents casting puzzled glances at me, then between themselves, they appeared too absorbed in their own exuberance to be overly concerned.

Sometimes, when I felt no one was looking, I'd steal into the living room, take the small box from beneath the tree, and stroke it gently, a smile tugging up the corners of my mouth.

The big day arrived. My father, distributing the presents as usual, kept glancing over at my mother, a bemused but constant smile tipping his lips. In my memory, they'd always had the ability to communicate without words and I was certain I knew what they both anticipated.

Finally all the gifts had been distributed, unwrapped, exclaimed over, and laid aside...all except the small box. The best for last I thought and wondered where they'd kept the puppy hidden. At our neighbor's?

That had to be it. Bob and Hilda loved dogs. Reassured I tried to will myself to stay calm and relax.

After what seemed like hours, my father picked up the little box. I held my breath.

"Gail," he said looking over at his wife, his expression mirroring all the happiness I was feeling in my soul. "Your mother and I have something to tell you."

Yes, yes, oh yes, please get on with it! My heart hammered. I was barely able to breathe.

"You're going to have a baby brother or sister this spring."

Astounded I could only gape at them. A bucket of ice water hitting me in the face couldn't have come as more of a shock. What was my father saying? I'd been an only child all my life. Now suddenly…

But then my father was handing me the little box.

"We know how much you love dogs…" he continued softly.

Apparently he and my mother had feared a negative response to their announcement and so had been saving the puppy presentation until afterwards. I revived sufficiently to tear off the wrappings, my prospective sibling instantly unimportant. They could have their baby; I'd have my dog.

I pawed through the tissue paper inside the box…where was that collar and leash?…and found at the bottom of it all a gold and white china dog.

My heart plummeted. I'm sure an x-ray taken at that moment would have shown it dropping floor-ward at the speed of light.

I held the cold bit of glass in my hands and looked up at my parents. Utter disappointment must have laid a pall over my face.

"I thought…" I let the dog fall back into its tissue paper bed. Overwhelmed by grief, I jumped to my feet and fled to my room.

My father found me there a half-hour later. He was carrying the china dog.

"I wanted a real dog!" I sobbed as I had for the past thirty minutes. "Nothing else! No baby, no china ornament! Just a real, live dog!"

"Gail, real dogs get old and die." My father's voice was soft. I remembered him telling me about the husky named Jack he'd had as a boy and the terrible pain he'd suffered when the old dog died. "I don't want you to get hurt. My father recited a bit of a poem to me just before I got Jack. I wish I'd paid attention. It went something like this, 'Brothers and sisters, I bid you beware; Of giving your heart to a dog to tear.' He was right."

"Oh, but Daddy, think of all the love and happiness in between!"

With a weary sigh, he took out his wallet, and handed me a crisp twenty-dollar bill. A child of the Great Depression he still believed money could heal a lot of ills.

"Buy whatever you want," he said resignedly handing it to me.

With a pang of guilt I realized I'd let my distress color what for him and my mother must have been a glorious time. They'd wanted another child for over a decade and now, finally, they would have one. I took the money, knowing to refuse it would only wound him further.

After he'd left my room, I sat down amid stacks of dog books, magazines and pictures and fingered the money absently. My father's words echoed back to me: "Buy whatever you want with it."

Suddenly, as it had so often done and would continue to do throughout my life, inspiration struck. The next morning, Boxing Day, I donned warm clothes and headed up the street to our town's only veterinarian's house.

"Dad, will you drive me to Douglastown tomorrow?" I asked him over supper that evening. I fancied my words trembled I was so full of a violent mix of trepidation and anticipation.

"Why?" he asked looking up from his turkey pot pie. "Do you have a friend you want to visit?"

"Yes, well…no…well, sort of. But not just visit. I want to bring him back here…to live."

Both my parents stopped eating and stared me.

"Live?" My mother, not easily daunted, this time obviously was.

"Yes." I drew a deep breath and summoned all my courage. "He's a puppy…half German Shepherd and half Collie…with something wrong with his tail. I bought him this afternoon."

Two forks clattered onto matching Christmas plates. I have never to this day been stared at so astoundedly.

"You what?" My father was the first to find words.

"You said I could buy anything I wanted with that twenty dollars." I felt alternately hot and cold, shaky and solid, but I'd come too far to turn back now. "So I went to see Dr. Jarvis. I told him I wanted to buy a Collie pup but he said a purebred would cost more than twenty dollars. He thought for a while, then he said he knew a lady in Douglastown who had one puppy left for sale. It was a German Shepherd/Collie mix. She might let me have him for twenty dollars because he'd been borne with a crooked tail. So he called her and she said, yes and I told her I'd pick him up tomorrow."

At that point I ran out of breath and words simultaneously. The tightness in my chest and throat had overwhelmed me. I could only glance from my mother to my father and then down at my plate. I couldn't bear to let them see my expression if they vetoed my purchase.

For the longest hiatus in the history of my twelve years, silence held our kitchen in its grip. Cars swished by on the street outside, the refrigerator started, and the furnace kicked in. I felt as if I would surely die if they didn't speak soon.

"You did say she could buy whatever she wanted," my mother said finally. "And we are having the baby. She deserves something special of her own, too. And you did say…"

My heartbeat began to upgrade from a weak flutter to a steady drumbeat.

"Yes, yes, I know what I said." My father got up and went to the stove to refill his teacup. He poured slowly while my pulse pounded in my ears. *Please, please, please*. My thoughts were a chant.

When he finally turned back toward the table, he paused, then sighed and let a cautious smile seep over his face.

"Okay," he said.

All but upsetting his tea, I leaped up and rushed to hug him to within inches of strangulation.

"Thank you, thank you, thank you!" I cried my joy so intense I didn't think I could bear it. "I promise I'll take care of him. You'll never have to do a thing…after you take me to Douglastown, that is."

The next morning we headed out to get my very own dog.

When I first saw Prince (as I'd already named him) I became a life-long believer in love at first sight. It didn't matter that he was the leftover of the litter because of his crooked tail. It didn't matter that he was one hundred percent German Shepherd except for his golden brown color. It only mattered that he was mine and I was his and we'd be friends as long as both of us lived. As a twelve-year-old hugging her first very-own puppy, I believed I was as close to nirvana as I'd ever be on this earth.

That spring, the spring I turned thirteen, my brother was borne. Our family was complete and happy.

But it was not to last. Six months later my mother was diagnosed with cancer. Two years later she died.

I overheard people commenting on how brave I was as I went about caring for my little brother and helping my aunt move into our home to become our housekeeper. My father, overwhelmed by grief, barely seemed to notice. He'd been in his late thirties when he'd married. I think he'd been afraid to give his heart to anyone. His mother had died young, leaving his father a life-long, grieving widower. And then, of course, there'd been Jack.

But then he'd met my mother and love must have overcome his fear of loss. The bond they'd formed had been deep and unfailing...until now. Immersed in sorrow, he left my brother in my aunt's care and me largely on my own.

During the day I appeared stoic, handling my grief well and with dignity. But at night alone in my room with Prince, I vented my sorrow. I'd put my arms around his neck and sob into his soft, warm coat as I clung to his broad, solid shoulders. The leftover puppy with the crooked tail never let me down. He'd snuggle close and let me release my sorrow for as long as I needed him by my side.

In the months and years that followed, Prince continued to be there for me. He shared the joys and pain of numerous teenage romances, long walks with a girl and later young woman with a penchant for thoughtful solitude, and the words read aloud from the pages of multiple Hilroy scribblers kept hidden under the bed of his aspiring-writer friend.

When my father slowly began to surface from the pain of my mother's passing, Prince unobtrusively moved in to companion him as well. Dad owned a service station downtown and often, while I was in school, Prince would accompany him to work.

Time passed. Finally, peacefully one year shortly before Christmas, he left us.

That evening I found my father sitting alone in the kitchen staring down at the dog collar he held clutched in his hands.

"You were right, Dad," I said my words choked with tears and bitterness. "Real dogs just die and break your heart. I should have been content with the china one."

He looked up at me, turning the worn collar over in his hands. There were tears in his eyes.

"No, you were right," he said softly. "You understood that all the love and joy that comes before is worth it."

A Pink Dress and a Promise

I'll never forget the Christmas I was sixteen. All I wanted was to have my mother attend my high school graduation the following year. She was suffering from ovarian cancer and although the expressions on the faces of other family members didn't offer much hope, I firmly believed she would recover and be there.

My mother and I had always enjoyed a special bond, perhaps because I'd been her only child for thirteen years. We'd shared a passionate love of books and reading. She'd read to me every day until I learned to master the skill myself. Afterwards she continued to share my love of stories by enthusing over my attempts at authorship. An amateur actress, she appeared in numerous local theatre productions. I grew up attending rehearsals and being able to mouth every line assigned to her on opening night.

I especially recall a small party held for the cast and crew one evening after a performance. My mother had bought a new pink dress for the occasion. In my six-year-old eyes, she looked like an angel.

When I was thirteen, my brother was borne. Six months later my mother was diagnosed with cancer. At first I didn't worry. After all, she was my mother. She'd never die and leave me. But as one year stretched to two and she grew thinner and often despondent due to heavy medication, thin shivers of fear began to haunt my days.

Two weeks before Christmas that year her condition worsened. I tried to deny the despair I saw mirrored in my father's face as we sat by her hospital bed. To strengthen the reality of her recovery I talked to her of the future, a future we'd share.

"And when you come to my graduation, will you wear your pink dress?" I asked her as she lay weak and thin on December 9th.

"Oh, honey, I don't know." She forced a hint of a smile. "That old thing? Really?"

"Yes, yes, please promise."

"All right, if that's what you really want…I promise." The words were barely above a whisper.

An hour later she passed away.

Somehow I forced myself through the next year and a half of school. My father had drifted away in his own world of grief. My aunt who came to take care of my two-year-old brother had no time for me. When graduation rolled around, both declined to attend.

As I sat on the platform with the other graduates, I felt hollow and utterly alone. I'd believed my mother would get well, I'd believed she'd be there for this milestone in my life. No one could possibly feel as bereft of happiness as I did at that moment.

Then the principal was announcing the prize for literature, for outstanding work in creative writing. The student on my right prodded me. "You won, you won!" she hissed.

Stunned I remained seated. And then I saw her. Standing at the back right hand corner of the auditorium, my mother, wearing the pink dress, was applauding vehemently.

I stood and made my way to the podium to collect

my award, all but staggering under the overwhelming sense of joy. She'd come. She'd promised and she'd come. And she was wearing the pink dress. The moments fluttered wildly in my heart, a beautiful butterfly of joy. In a cloud of happiness so intense I could barely control my movements, I returned to my seat. But when I looked at the back right hand corner of thc room she was gone.

Later as I walked home alone in the soft, warm darkness of the spring evening, my award and diploma clasped in my hand, my attitude changed. Anger suffused me. Why had she come only for an instant? Why couldn't she have stayed?

I sat down on a park bench by the river and stared at the calm water. Slowly understanding came. She couldn't always be with me, not anymore, but she would be there when I needed her most. She'd kept her promise, hadn't she. She'd worn the pink dress.

Without Words

So many Christmas memories warm my heart during the Yuletide season but those of the times spent with my paternal grandfather and sharing the deep and abiding love we had for dogs and horses are in a class by themselves.

Granddad was deaf. Not stone deaf but sufficiently hearing impaired to make communicating with him a chore. He stubbornly refused to wear the hearing aid the family had purchased. It was more bother than it was worth he'd mutter. Frustrated in his attempts to interpret what was said he became gruff, taciturn, and withdrawn.

Most of the family, equally frustrated, minimized their conversations with him. Left largely on his own, Granddad turned to the dogs and horses that had always been a big part of his *raison d'etre* and *joie de vivre*.

A shy, introverted child who preferred the written to the spoken word and an equally passionate canine and equine fancier, I fit hand in glove as Granddad's companion. Each Sunday afternoon when my parents and I visited his farm, he and I would slip away from the cacophony of the family gathering in the big country kitchen. Without a single word passing between us, we'd saunter out to the barn, Granddad's dog at our heels.

Once inside we'd stroll past the cow stalls filled with large-eyed Jerseys in winter, empty in summer, then sit down on a bench against the wall beside the horse stalls. Granddad's pair of Percherons, Smiler and Lou, would back their great haunches until they could turn their head and roll big brown eyes at their visitors. They'd whinny a soft welcome, then return to their hay-filled mangers.

Granddad would pull a couple of oranges from his mackinaw pocket and hand one to me. In companionable silence we'd peel and eat.

When we'd finished, Granddad would go to the back door that accessed the pasture and throw it wide open. The horses, in anticipation, would stop munching and begin to move restlessly. Slapping them on the rumps to get them to move aside, he'd go into their stalls and release first one, then the other.

With eager snorts and dancing hooves, they'd back themselves free, whirl, and thunder out of the barn, iron-clad hooves echoing over the plank floor.

From the doorway, Granddad and I would watch them race away, tails and manes streaming, spirited beauty on the hoof, over brilliant green grass in summer and glistening snow in winter. Glancing up into Granddad's bright blue eyes, I knew he shared my joy in those moments that were perfect for both of us.

Sometimes we watched them for nearly an hour, not a single word passing between us. Then, as the time for me to go home grew near, Granddad would call out to them. No matter how far out across the pasture the team happened to be at that moment, they'd pause, turn, and prick their ears in his direction. He'd call again and they'd start toward him at a trot, thick necks arched, obedient out of love and respect for the man by my side.

I was thirteen that winter and totally enamored with

horses and dependent on those Sunday afternoon visits to shore up my spirits for the week ahead at junior high school. To this day the scent of oranges still sends my spirit back to those wonderful afternoons with Granddad.

Glowing from my time with Granddad and the horses, I returned to the farmhouse late one November afternoon in time to catch my ride home with my parents. My heart and mind occupied with flying manes and tails and sleek, powerful creatures of incredible beauty, I paid little attention to the discussion between my uncle who had taken over the farm from my eighty-year-old Granddad and my father.

"…horses cost a lot to keep over the winter. We won't be logging with them this year either. A tractor…"

I climbed into the backseat and closed the door on my uncle's words. I wasn't worried. Granddad and his horses were as much a part of the farm as the orchards and meadows.

Then came the Sunday just before Christmas. A still, hard frost gripped a still, gray morning when I awoke. As my parents and I drove toward Granddad's farm shortly after noon I gazed out the window at the bare, brown, barren landscape of a winter's day laying in wait for the first snow to give it life and sparkle.

I hoped there'd be snow soon; snow deep enough and soft enough for Smiler and Lou to gallop through, sprays of white crystals flying from their pounding hooves. *Maybe it would snow later that day.*

At the farm I jumped out of the car and headed for the barn at a run.

"Tell Granddad I'm out here," I yelled back over

my shoulder to my parents.

I unlatched the door and hurried past the row of placidly munching Jerseys. And stopped short.

The horses' stall stood empty. And clean. Pristinely clean. Hosed and scrubbed clean. A horrible sense of unreality swept over me. My uncle's words resounded in my mind. I felt lightheaded, my stomach roiled. *No! No! No!*

"Smiler! Lou!" I yelled dashing to the rear door and flinging it open. The pasture with its frost-dead grass lay silent and empty...except for a shiny red tractor parked near the back of the barn.

"No!" My cry echoed its despair out across the field. "No!"

I heard the front door open. I turned to see Granddad coming inside. He seemed to have shrunken from his lofty six-foot-four-inch height, his broad shoulders stooped as he came slowly down the length of the barn toward me. As he drew near, I saw that his blue eyes were faded, their sparkle gone.

When he reached our bench he sat down heavily and looked up at me. His eyes filled with tears and so did mine. I sank down beside him and scrubbed them away with the backs of my mittens. He dug into his mackinaw pocket, pulled out two oranges and handed one to me.

I took it. Holding the unpeeled fruit in our hands, we sat silently side by side and watched the first flakes of winter begin to obliterate the hoof prints churned into the earth outside the back door of the barn.

I didn't realize it at the time, my pain being too deep and acute, but in later years I'd recognize the wonderful memories those days with Granddad had made, the hours spent in companionable silence, the sharing of beauty and freedom that spoke louder than words and would forever help me find the beauty of Christmas in my heart.

Granddad and His Dog

The special bond Granddad and I had didn't end with the loss of the horses. I continued to visit him and share what sometimes amounted to mostly silent but nevertheless important moments together.

One snowy Christmas Eve shortly after Granddad had found himself alone in the big, white farm house on the hill, I discovered him leaning on the mailbox post by the gate. Gram had died many years previous and one by one his children and grandchildren had drifted away. Buster, his Collie/St. Bernard mix stood by his side, his head drooping. Were they remembering fuller, happier times I wondered as I stopped my car beside the old man in the dipper cap and plaid mackinaw.

The dog shook ermine flakes from his woolly coat and wagged his busy tail slowly as he recognized me. His muzzle had grown as gray as Granddad's stubble. It had been too long since I'd visited them.

"Granddad, hop in," I shouted reaching across to shove open the passenger door. Granddad still refused to wear his hearing aid. "Merry Christmas, Buster. Get in the back, will you, buddy?"

"Let him ride in front," my grandfather said opening the door for the old dog. "He likes to see where he's going."

The bond between Granddad and his dog had always been obvious. I recall him sitting in the twilight by a long, narrow farmhouse window on a blanket-covered couch beside a big wood stove in the kitchen, reading "The Family Herald," shabby carpet slippers on his feet, granny glasses perched midway down his nose. Buster sat beside him, resting his muzzle on the shoulder of his companion's faded plaid shirt.

As I matured I began to see Granddad's handicap as part of the reason he preferred the company of his dog. He didn't have to struggle to comprehend or concern himself about making an inappropriate response.

Buster was to be the last in a line of canines that lived out long, contented lives under my grandfather's guidance and guardianship. When Granddad, aged eighty, had purchased the pup, my father had deemed it a ridiculous move.

"Father won't live much longer and then we'll have to find a home for a big farm pup," he'd declared, shaking his head ruefully.

But live much longer he did. Granddad had turned ninety-six that Christmas I met him at the gate. Buster was a venerable sixteen.

Granddad had trained Buster as he had all his dogs in their youth to herd and guard, to respect and obey. I never saw him hug a dog but then I never saw him physically punish one either.

"You'd better go down and bring those cows up now," I recall him telling Buster on summer evenings when I was visiting the farm. And off the dog would go, to reappear shortly over the crest of the hill, driving the herd in for milking at the proper slow plod.

As time passed, Buster became Granddad's ears. He let him know when someone was coming up the hill to the house or knocking at the door or when a weasel threatened the chicken coop.

Buster rode on the seat of the truck wagon with Granddad on work days and in his buggy (which my grandfather insisted on driving well into the 1960's) with him on Sundays. About the only time they were separated was when Granddad went to town and then Buster spent his day at the gate, waiting for his return and guarding the property.

Granddad died that spring. Buster, matted and arthritic, stood in a corner of the front verandah, shaggy head drooping, as the coffin was carried out of the rambling old house and down the steps.

The following morning I found the old dog seemingly asleep by the long window in the kitchen. His head rested on a pair of shabby carpet slippers. All of his life he'd demonstrated the spirit of Christmas through his loyalty, love, and devotion. What more could anyone expect of a relationship.

Angel in a Kerchief

Angels walk among us. They appear unexpectedly, not exclusively during the Christmas season, but always when they're needed most. Sometimes they even wear a kerchief.

This particular angel came to me in February but since she was the embodiment of the true spirit of Christmas, her story belongs in this collection. This is the story of my own special angel...

A blizzard was raging outside the small Tabusintac farm house my new husband and I had moved in to three days earlier. As I looked out the window into the roiling sea of white, I felt lost and alone. Married only a week, Ron and I had moved to this small, rural community where he taught school and I, a newcomer, knew virtually no one. I'd made a terrible mistake, I thought, and wanted desperately to go home to my widower father. I was nineteen.

As tears trickled down my cheeks, I saw something moving out in the storm. Then I realized it was a person struggling through the wind and snow, a kerchief tied about her head and a package tucked under her arm. Who would come out on such a terrible day I wondered as my visitor battled her way onto my doorstep.

"Hello," she said when I opened the door to be greeted by a gust of wind and snow and the sweetest smile this side of heaven. "I'm Maud Hierlihy, your neighbor from across the road. I thought you might like a loaf of fresh bread."

"Come in," I invited taking the package from her. Its warmth spread into my cold hands.

She removed the wet kerchief from her graying hair. "Thank you," she said, still smiling.

As she bent to pull off her snow-crusted boots, a sense of peace and belonging wafted over me. The desire to go back to my former home began to shrink.

Eighteen months later, Maud would again make another of what had become regular visits to our small house, this time to minister to my baby daughter who was screaming until her tiny face had turned a horrible shade of red. I believe I was in a worse state than the child, terrified and feeling utterly helpless. Maud took Joan in her arms, sat down in a rocking chair, laid her gently face-down across her knees and began to massage her back.

Within seconds a huge belch erupted from the tiny body, and Joan stopped crying.

"Sometimes putting a child over your shoulder doesn't work," she smiled gently up at me. "Sometimes this does."

The mother of eight, Maud knew what she was talking about.

The next spring Maud again crossed the back country road to our house to take Joan home with her while I went to the hospital to give birth to her sister, Carol. There was a repeat performance the following year when our son Steven was born. Each time I went into the delivery room secure in the knowledge that my family couldn't have been in better hands.

Never a rich woman, Maud, a farmer's wife, always

had an extra bottle of homemade jam, block of freshly churned butter, bag of apples, or pork roast to give to friends and neighbors. The idea of payment never entered her mind.

Throughout the years she was always unobtrusively there when I needed her. She helped out when I was sick, nurtured my spirit when I despaired, and became surrogate grandmother to my children. She made the best molasses cookies "in the whole wide world" Joan declared when she began to talk. Hihi, as she called Maud, was the fairy godmother who took her picking blueberries and let her play among her chickens.

When Maud Hierlihy died at the age of eighty-six, the entire population of Tabusintac turned out to mourn her passing. She'd seldom traveled beyond the boundaries of the small rural community where she'd been born and lived all her life, had never become rich or famous but within the little service district she called home, her kindness and altruism had become legendary.

A month later my beloved dog, Chance, died. Maud would have known how to comfort me I thought, my heart aching as I stored Chance's collar in a drawer. She would have known what to do to ease my pain and loneliness.

That night I had a dream. I saw Maud, a kerchief tied around her head, picking blueberries in a beautiful, sun-drenched meadow. Chance sat at her side. An aura of peace surrounded them. The ache in my heart subsided, soothed by the vision of an angel who carried the spirit of Christmas in her heart every day of the year.

Twelve-Month Santa

Another Christmas memory embedded deep in my heart is, in my opinion, better than the exploits of Santa and Rudolph. It's the story of a mail carrier and his horse, the true story of Edgar Hierlihy and his faithful mare Peg. Maud's husband, he, like his wife, was blessed with an altruistic spirit. In the thirteen years (1951-1964) he and Peg delivered the post in the small rural New Brunswick community of Tabusintac, they brought so much more than the mail to the scattered homes along their route that they far exceeded the expectations held for Santa. Furthermore, they did it not just once in December but six times a week, twelve months of the year.

Quite possibly the last mail carrier in New Brunswick to deliver using actual horsepower, Edgar distributed a cornucopia of items Canada Post would never have approved. Settled into the back of his wagon, huddled between mail bags were groceries, pints of cream, jugs of milk, cartons of eggs, bricks of butter, dress patterns, and, in season, flower bulbs and seeds.

Edgar carried the news of the community to the scattered farms along his route, as well. Never too rushed to share a sorrow, a joke, or a cup of tea, he brought a boundless supply of information and good will that connected his community regardless of weather or road conditions.

"These back country roads in spring could be a combination of mud, slush, and frozen ruts," Edgar's son-in-law Boucher Palmer recalled. "Under those conditions, Edgar would borrow a second horse from his neighbor and harness her beside Peg to make a team. Then he'd hitch them to a drag sled and head out along his route."

Spring was also the time Edgar delivered special items such as the first crop of rhubarb. Like a harbinger of summer, he brought bundles to anyone who had a taste for it along his route.

May and June would find him delivering those all-important orders from Eaton's catalogue. Outfits for weddings, christenings, and graduations crowded into Edgar's buggy. In late summer and autumn, he brought new clothes for back-to-school. And, of course, just before Christmas, he delivered packages containing gifts and items that would be gifts.

Along his route, he also carried out numerous services Canada Post would never have dreamed of including in a job description. He delivered lunches forgotten at home to children in any of several of the one-room schools along his way and drove students who felt sick back home.

"I remember Edgar picking me up at school one day when I was about seven years old," recalled Carol Robertson. "I was feeling terrible and just wanted to go home. It was winter, and Edgar tucked me into the buffalo robe he had in his sleigh. To this day I'm grateful for that drive. I found out later I had pneumonia."

"Whenever I needed a drive to school, Edgar and Peg would pick me up and drive me," Mary (Ross)

Stokes, a teacher at one of the single classroom schools along Edgar's route, remembered. "To offer to pay him would have been to insult him. Doing favors was a way of life for him."

And all this for $2.50 a day. Later, under contract, he'd make $20.00 a week. Included in this princely sum was the assumption that he'd provide his own means of transportation.

"When oats went to $3.20 a bag, Dad didn't know how he could afford to continue," his son Frank said. "He always took good care of Peg and wouldn't see her go to work without being properly fed.

"Sometimes Dad used another horse to give Peg a break but generally it was Peg who did the mail route," Frank continued. "We estimate Peg had over 52,000 miles on her when, due to illness, she had to be put down. She was born on our farm and lived out her entire life there. The day she left us was a sad one."

Frank recalled his father coming home from his mail route and after he and the faithful Peg had eaten their supper, both of them heading out to help a neighboring widow with her haying.

Edgar's dedication to assisting friends and neighbors appeared boundless. Residents still tell the story of how he returned to the local grocery store on the main road to get a special kind of milk for a baby whose family had no means of transportation. And this was after a full day of delivering mail…a day that had started at 9:00 am with sorting at the post office and, on a good day, ended at 3:00 pm.

"There was no backup for Dad," Frank said. "No sick days or anything like that. Dad drove the mail no matter how he felt. I remember in winter he wore an old fur coat with a parka and woolen mitts with leather covers. He always wore a tie pulled up tight to help him keep warm and had a couple of buffalo robes to throw over his knees. Nothing kept him from his rounds. He was dedicated to his job."

But perhaps the most appreciated and unfailing service Edgar provided was his willingness to lend an empathetic ear. No matter how long or demanding his day, no matter how tired he might be, he always had time to sympathize with a problem and share a joke. His sense of humor brightened many moments for customers along his route.

Edgar could just as easily laugh at his own foibles as he could at someone else's. One local classic example concerned the day the local minister asked Edgar for a drive across the Tabusintac Bridge.

With his usual alacrity, Edgar replied, "Sure, sure."

What Edgar didn't know was that while he and the minister had been chatting in the post office, some of the local pranksters had fastened a large, provocative picture of a lady inside the front of his buggy. It had been intended as an innocuous bit of humor since they'd had no way of knowing the clergyman was going to ask for a lift.

When Edgar emerged with the minister, they could only watch as he and his unexpected passenger proceeded to the buggy and climbed aboard.

Although history hasn't recorded what happened next, anyone who knew Edgar could predict. He'd mutter a few startled, "Dear, dears," flap the reins to put Peg into motion, and proceed to view the incident exactly in the way in which it was intended...an affectionate joke on a man everyone knew was perfectly capable of appreciating it.

He enjoyed any well-intentioned story that could get a laugh. A favorite concerned one of his pigs. When it got out of its pen and was found wandering on the road near his farm he'd deny ownership. It was just too darned ugly he chuckled.

And then there was the tale about his cow. When he met a local lady on the road one afternoon as he was leading Bessie home from having made her annual visit to a neighbor's bull, he told her the Jersey had run away rather than risk offending the woman's delicate sensibilities.

Edgar Hierlihy retired from delivering the mail in 1964 at age sixty-five. When he passed away on September 4, 1976, the entire community turned out for his funeral.

"I can't remember anyone ever having a bad word to say about Dad," Frank said softly.

There's an old Irish saying that goes something to the effect that you should live your life so well that when you die, even the undertaker is sorry. And he was. Edgar, the twelve-month Santa Claus, had lived the kind of life that could make it happen and left his memory strong in my heart.

The Night of the Northern Lights

Time passed and our family expanded to include three bright, delightful, lively (forgive the description but I *am* their mother) children. Our own family traditions grew as well. One of them was an annual week-after-Christmas visit to our camp. It was a much anticipated event for the kids but one cold, blustery December day as we loaded our Volkswagon Beetle for the trek, I wondered if it was worth the effort. Piling enough boots, jackets, bedding, and groceries into a miniscule car with three kids (ages eight, nine, and ten) and two dogs (a Lab and a Beagle) was a monumental task. As husband, Ron, fastened skis, poles, and snowshoes on the roof, I looked at the kids, their faces bright with anticipation and decided, *okay, just one more year*. Christmas with its commercialism and financial stress had worn me to the "bah humbug" stage that winter.

Once packed and everyone in place, wiggle room was close to non-existent. No one dared ask for a pit stop, not even the dogs. Their heads protruding from among clothing, sleeping bags, and food, quite possibly only the anticipation of the country freedom kept them quiet.

Volkswagens of those days were supposedly kept snug as the proverbial bug in a rug by a gas heater. Ours invariably failed during those Yuletide trips. Only overcrowding and body heat saved us from hypothermia.

Finally we arrived at the camp to an orange-pink sunset slashed with purple brushstrokes above a snow frosted forest of spruce and pines. We huddled together on the doorstep while Ron unlocked the door.

Bursting into the interior, we discovered the place felt colder than outdoors. While Ron ignited the oil space heater in the cabin's center, the children and I scrambled to divest the overburdened car. The dogs, wild after their release, raced through the snowdrifts.

A half hour later, in the slowly warming room, we boiled wieners on a camp stove and softened half-frozen buns in the steam. As darkness fell, an oil lamp illuminated sleeping bags spread out on the bunks. Outside skis, poles, and snowshoes leaned ready against the wall beside a cooler that kept milk, eggs, meat, and butter from spoiling in a dwelling as yet unacquainted with refrigeration.

Traditionally, after we ate, we made a trek on snowshoes down to the river. However, on this particular night, Ron and the girls opted to try out three pairs of spanking new cross country skis over the meadow. That left Steve, the dogs and me for the river foray. With a full moon at our backs, we started off.

Our shadows stretched before us, elongated and mobile. The dogs cavorted in and out of the darkness of trees that snapped and crackled in the frost. An occasional mutter from Steve, as we tramped along, reaffirmed he still wasn't happy with our second choice excursion.

We paused as we reached the bank above the river and suddenly...magic. Shy at first, then gradually sprouting higher and higher up among the stars in the night sky, the Northern Lights appeared. Undulating like mystic spirits gowned in green and white, they rose and rose, then doubled back on themselves to rise again. The heavens danced, alive with their essence.

I glanced down at Steve. With the dogs sitting by his side, he stared spellbound.

In the Far North, people say they've heard the Northern Lights speak in the whistling voice of migratory birds. Auroras, they claim, are sent to buoy up people's spirits during the long winter when the sun doesn't shine.

Apparently they had the same effect on my son.

"Wow!" he breathed, delighted astonishment erasing all traces of discontent.

No neon display could equal it. "Bah humbug" faded from my thoughts, the wonder that is Christmas reviving in my heart in the presence of this, truly one of nature's priceless gifts.

When the mystic dance finally began to recede, we turned and headed back to the camp. The enchanted lights of the winter night would fade from the sky but never from my memory or that of the entranced boy by my side. Those magical moments in the moonlight would live forever within us, one we could never have experienced if we hadn't made that annual Yuletide trek to the camp. Now, each year, their memory helps revive the magic of Christmas in my heart.

The Fifty-Cent Angel

Sometimes precious Christmas memories come in unusual packages. Thirty years ago my husband, Ron, and I bought a gold-colored celluloid angel to top our Christmas tree. She came from a reduced-to-clear bin in a local department store and cost fifty cents. Our children, three-year-old Steve, four-year-old Carol, and five-year-old Joan, were agog at her shimmering beauty held triangularly erect by a cardboard underskirt. She had a gentle face, gleaming yellow hair, and a glistening pipe cleaner halo. She was "just beautiful" they breathed when we brought her home.

Ron and I didn't plan to keep the angel. She was only a stopgap until we could afford a more elegant tree top decoration. Nevertheless the years passed and each December Ron continued to carefully place the ornament we'd named The-Fifty-Cent-Angel at the top of our balsam fir while three children with glowing faces watched.

The-Fifty-Cent-Angle watched, too. During the lean years, she looked on as Ron and I worried that the gifts we could afford would prove disappointments to the children. She'd also seen our relief when our trio joyfully accepted our offerings as if they were state-of-the-art.

Presumably she witnessed Santa's many visits. Her smile may even have broadened a bit as she cast her golden glow down on his kindly deeds.

But not all our Christmas's were merry and bright. One year my father passed away in mid-December. His death left an excruciating void in my soul. Although Ron and I definitely weren't in a festive mood, we put up a tree for the kids' sake and tried to make the best of a painful situation.

At midnight, a week later, after everyone else in the house was asleep, I could no longer contain my grief. I left the bed and went into the living room to curl up in the rocking chair beside the evergreen. Looking up at the tree, I wept. Nothing stayed the same I thought bitterly. Life was only a hodgepodge of heartbreaking changes. A dear, gentle man had gone out of my life forever and my world had become a cold, lonely place. The garishly trimmed tree seemed absolutely inappropriate.

Then something gently gleaming in the darkness caught my attention. Through my tears I looked up and saw her gazing down on me. Glowing in the reflected illumination of the street light outside our window, The-Fifty-Cent-Angel gazed down to remind me of another Christmas; a Christmas with a smiling grandfather watching three rambunctious youngsters tumbling around in freshly fallen snow and grinning over their exploits.

Suddenly I knew that those beautiful, loving memories would remain forever in my heart and that as long as they did, my father would never leave my life.

My pain drained away. Peace descended over me.

Time passed. The kids became teenagers. It seemed that there was no common ground between our offspring and us. Nothing Ron or I said was sufficiently cool to warrant their interest. We'd become strangers to our own children, as alien as if we'd just landed from Mars.

Christmas arrived. Ron and I trimmed the tree alone for the first time. Our hearts not really in the task, we forgot to place The-Fifty-Cent-Angel on its top.

When the kids arrived home from a movie, they barely acknowledged our efforts. When they saw The-Fifty-Cent-Angel on a table, however, all blasé indifference vanished.

"What's wrong? Why isn't The-Fifty-Cent-Angel on the tree?"

Steve was handing her to his father while Carol and Joan pulled the stepladder into position. "We can't have Christmas without The-Fifty-Cent-Angel!"

When she finally stood atop the balsam fir, all five of us stepped back to admire her…once again.

"Remember the Christmas…" Joan began and suddenly we were all reminiscing about Yuletide's past.

More time passed. The kids finished high school and moved on to university. When all three had completed their studies, Ron and I brought a new treetop ornament, a glowing electric star. It would symbolize a milestone in our financial lives…we thought.

The moment Joan, Carol, and Steve arrived home for the holidays and saw the new decoration, there was a simultaneous outcry. Within minutes The-Fifty-Cent-Angel had been pulled from a pile of discarded decorations in the basement. Her crooked, pipe cleaner halo was lovingly straightened, a tear in her skirt carefully mended with scotch tape. Then, proudly, reverently, she was once again handed to Ron to be returned to her place atop the bushy fir.

More time passed. Jobs and partners drew the

children away from home. Ron and I found ourselves among that segment of society known as empty nesters. Our first Christmas alone arrived. With the help of The-Fifty-Cent-Angel, the memories she held in her aging celluloid body, and three lengthy long-distance telephone calls, we managed to get through a much quieter holiday season.

Finally a December came when I found myself alone in our house. Ron was in the hospital scheduled for by-pass surgery. My thoughts occupied elsewhere, I wasn't eager to get out any of our seasonal decorations. The idea of Christmas trimming seemed frivolous under the circumstances.

Finally, upon reflection, I modified my position. Ron had always loved the holidays and their resultant decorations. It would be disloyal of me not to acknowledge the season on his behalf. With this in mind, I went out and purchased a tree. I brought it home, pulled the boxes of balls and tinsel from the attic, and began to trim its branches.

When I came to The-Fifty-Cent-Angel, I paused. Carefully I lifted the old cherub from her tissue paper bedding and looked into her kindly, aged face.

"You'll have to wait," I said and placed her on a table by the window.

Two weeks later, I handed her to Ron and watched as, a bit shakily but traditionally, he mounted the stepladder to place her atop the tree.

Last year our two-year-old grandson arrived to spend Christmas with us. Eyes wide with wonder, he gazed at the glittering tree. Then he watched as his grandfather placed The-Fifty-Cent-Angel on its top. His face lit up with sudden, enchanted joy. Eagerly he stretched small hands out toward it.

"Grammie and Grampie brought The-Fifty-Cent-Angel home when I wasn't much older than you," his dad, Steve, explained, lifting his son up to get a better look. "She's been our family angel ever since."

Our family angel. I'd never thought of her in those terms but I realized it was true. An integral part of the magic and memories that define Christmas in our home, the Fifty-Cent Angel from a department store bargain bin has become priceless.

An Owl Named Santa Claws

Christmas memories that lodge in the heart can be born in unusual places. This one came to life in a little country cemetery one cold December day shortly before the onset of the Yuletide season.

As the minister began to read Uncle Abner's eulogy, a cold, gray mist drifted in off the bay to add to the gloom of the bitterly cold winter afternoon. It gave the little country cemetery an air of bleakness. I thought of the man in the casket before me. The hastily purchased dark suit, white shirt, and navy tie he wore had made him a stranger to me.

"Earth to earth, ashes to ashes, dust to dust; in sure and certain hope of the Resurrection into eternal life," the clergyman recited the time-worn words.

I stood beside the open grave and remembered Uncle Abner as I'd known him. All I'd ever seen him wear was a baggy salt-and-pepper peaked cap, patched gum boots, too-large woolen work pants held up by a pair of frayed suspenders, and a faded plaid flannel shirt, the top of his long johns peeking out at neck and sleeves. He'd always seemed small and bent, his weathered face permanently crinkled from too many good-natured grins.

He'd never gone to school long enough to learn to read or write, but he'd managed to survive for seventy-plus years without that knowledge. Daybreak, sunset, and autumn were among his favorite things.

He'd never held a nine-to-five job or gotten a regular pay check. But then he'd never had a car payment or a mortgage or an ulcer, either. And he'd never collected welfare, unemployment benefits, or any other kind of government handout.

Uncle Abner had simply been a farmer of sorts most of his life. Neighbors laughed and poked fun at his easy-going lifestyle, shaking their heads over his weather-beaten house and barn and at the chickens that ate pet-like from his hand on the front porch.

And when his boar, through some mysterious illness, lost all his teeth and Uncle Abner refused to have him put down, another farmer couldn't resist nudging him about it.

"Does it bother old Samson, not havin' any choppers?" he asked Uncle Abner one day as the pair leaned against the pigpen watching the big animal root about in his milk-filled trough.

"Only when he smiles," he replied stony-faced.

My uncle never owned a car. He was often seen walking along the dusty roads near his farm, limping a little when his lumbago acted up, accompanied by Bob his pet crow. Bob was lame, too. Uncle Abner had rescued the bird from being stoned to death by a group of small boys, taken him home, and nursed him back to health. But Bob's leg would never be the same again.

When neighbors encountered Uncle Abner and Bob limping toward home, they'd pull over and offer a ride. Uncle Abner gratefully accepted but not before telling Bob to, "Fly on home. I'll meet you there directly."

Bob was only one of many permanent and semi-permanent guests at the farm. My uncle had a way of collecting injured and deserted wild creatures from the fields and river to swell the livestock population of his homestead. I remember him nursing a raccoon named Joseph back to health after an encounter with a trap had crippled the animal's hind leg. Then there was George the Canada goose that lingered too long on the pond below Uncle Abner's house one autumn and had to be cut, half-starved, from the ice. George spent the winter safe and warm in my uncle's barn. In the spring, when migrating flocks returned, George rejoined his friends.

Most poignantly, I remember the winter Uncle Abner kept the Great Snowy Owl. He'd found the bird stunned by a hunter's shotgun pellet on the boundary of his property and brought it home. With food and care it recovered quickly; by Christmas week it was almost well enough to leave.

Three days before Christmas a trophy collector arrived at the farm. He wanted the owl…dead and stuffed…for his den.

"They're a rare species around here," he explained. "I'll meet any reasonable price you ask."

My uncle glanced over at his three children. There weren't many gifts that year. But, then, there never were. The kids could use new boots. My Aunt Anna, hovered at his elbow while her husband rubbed his stubbly chin.

"Rare, eh?" he said reflectively.

Slowly he stooped forward and released the catch on the cage door. Startled, Aunt Anna and the collector ran for the safety of the back porch.

The great bird hesitated a moment. Then it blinked, shook itself, and stretched its magnificent wings. Seconds later it floated silently past the pair on the verandah and up into the snowy sky. Uncle Abner raised a hand in farewell salute.

"Good-bye, Santa Claws," he said.

The next morning a green grocer, desperate for vegetables to fill holiday orders, arrived at the farm. My uncle's root cellar was full of carrots, turnips, beets, and potatoes. The kids got their boots.

That was many Christmas's ago. Now Uncle Abner's children are grown. All three have left the farm and distinguished themselves. Jack, his eldest, has become a biologist intent on wildlife conservation; Janet, his only daughter, is a doctor; Robert, his second boy, attended agricultural college and is developing new methods of growing organic crops. I looked across the coffin and saw how deeply they had loved and respected their father reflected in their bereaved expressions.

Suddenly the sun broke through the fog and turned the mist into a glistening silver veil, the bare-limbed birches into diamond-studded webs. From the shimmering pines on the edge of the cemetery, a robin burst into song.

Foolish bird, I thought. *You should have gone south by now*.

I glanced up into the golden white sky and remembered a great owl rising silently into the gently falling flakes of Christmas. I thought about a goose named George and a raccoon named Joseph and a crow named Bob and a robin lingering to sing at a funeral.

The minister finished speaking and closed his Bible. I had my last glimpse of the simple, brown coffin as it was lowered into the waiting earth. Then, turning from the grave, I took the arm of the woman standing by my side.

"Come on, Aunt Anna. It's time to go home. I have a story to write about an owl named Santa Claws."

Christmas Confessions

Another Christmas memory that has found a very special niche in my heart concerns my beloved father-in-law, Wilson MacMillan. In 1939, as an eighteen-year-old husband and father of an infant son, he was one of thousands of young men who gave up the comforts and joys of life in Canada to go to fight for king, country, and freedom.

Private Wilson Joseph MacMillan left his New Brunswick home and family to become a gunner, an infantryman to fight in the heat, cold, dirt, and terror of foreign front lines.

I first met Wilson (or Wit as he was nicknamed) in 1962. He appeared one of the happiest, most contented men I'd ever encountered, at peace with both himself and the world.

His demeanor puzzled me. Husband Ron had told me he'd spent four horrific years between 1941 and 1945 in the front lines of the European Theatre of World War II. How had it been possible for him to put those traumatic times behind him and go on with his life?

He never talked about his war time experiences. Those memories appeared sealed, like top secret documents, deep inside the vault that was his heart. Sealed, that is, until several years after I'd become his daughter-in-law. As he and I sat alone in front of the wood stove in our den one blustery Christmas evening, I cautiously broached the subject of those years.

"No one wants to hear old war stories." He shifted in his chair and took another sip of his scotch.

"I do. I want to be able to tell your grandchildren. They have to know. It's important."

I stood and went to put another log on the fire. Flames and sparks crackled upward. As I glanced back at my father-in-law in their cavorting shadows I saw his expression changing, sliding into one of remembrance...and a struggle to face it.

I sat down and waited.

"I remember once when I was serving in Italy I was so hungry I traded my overcoat for two eggs." His lips curled into a small smile. "Then there was the time one of my buddies decided to shock an aristocratic British lady by showing her just exactly where he'd been wounded on the left buttock."

At first the stories followed these vain, light-hearted avoidances, anecdotes about pranks and escapades beyond the realm of commanding officers. Then slowly they began to change. As the fire died to embers other memories emerged, memories of horrific bombardments, of heat and cold and pain and terror, of lost friends and fallen comrades.

"I remember the night we attacked at Monte Cassino," he said, his gaze on the dying fire. "The Abbey of Monte Cassino was a monastery in southern Italy that had been built on the top of a mountain by St. Benedict in the sixth century. The German troops holed up in it had been impossible to rout. From their vantage point high up in that fortress-like structure, they could watch our every move. It was like laying siege to a medieval castle."

I recalled textbook accounts of the four horrific engagements fought over a five-month period from January to May of 1944 for possession of Monte Cassino. The Allies had decided to make a concentrated attack on the Abbey before most of their troops were shipped off to take part in the invasion of Normandy. It had been a massive operation with armed forces from over thirty countries participating.

The capture of Monte Cassino had been vital in order to free Allied troops trapped in northern Italy to link up with their comrades in the south and together march on Rome. After the Abbey was overwhelmed, that city became the first Axis capital to fall to the Allies on June 4, 1944.

I broke off my thoughts. Wit was speaking again.

"Under cover of darkness, without any lights and nearly no noise, massive numbers of men and incredible amounts of equipment were moved into the valley below the mountain," he said softly. "When the order to attack came, although it was midnight, the entire place lighted up like high noon."

Later research would inform me that the 1st Canadian Corps had been involved in the last of the battles for Monte Cassino in May 1944. Its assignment had been to take advantage of the breakthrough made by allied forces. It had been the 2nd Polish Corps who'd actually scaled the walls of the fortress and destroyed it at an incredible cost in human life.

Wit paused and gazed into the glowing coals. When he continued it was slowly and carefully, as if he was trying to find a way to tell a story that had been inside too long. "I remember another time in Italy…we were watching a farm house from the cover of some trees.

Germans had been reported hiding out in it." He stopped and closed his eyes for a moment before going on. "Suddenly a little girl about twelve or thirteen burst out of that house and started running toward us. We yelled at her to go back…but she just kept coming. Then shots erupted out of that house." The words trailed off. He didn't have to finish.

There was a silence. I got up and added a stick to the last of the fire.

"Still you never seemed to carry any animosity toward the enemy," I said sitting down again. "I've never heard you say a bitter word against the German troops."

"I remember my first night on duty in Italy." The explanation came slowly, quietly as he stared down into his glass. "They had sent me out to guard a huge anti-aircraft gun. I was nineteen years old, all alone in the dark with only my rifle. I was terrified. Later I realized that most of the German soldiers must have been just like me…young and scared to death. We were all in it together. The war wasn't any more their fault than it was mine. We were all just doing our duty."

I looked over at this remarkable man who'd had the strength to prevent personal animosity from eroding his spirit, even in the face of death, and knew I'd glimpsed a part of what, much more than the medals he'd won, made him a hero.

Perhaps this philosophy and his having the strength to live according to it had proven an inspiration to his comrades. Certainly at his funeral in 1990, the men of his old regiment exhibited a profound respect and affection for their fellow soldier.

Wit had refused promotions to stay with his buddies

fighting at the front. Some of them may have followed his example. Whatever the reason, they'd remained his life-long friends.

But it was only last Remembrance Day, I came to understand what I believe had sustained my father-in-law during those horrendous years, what had made it possible for him to return to Canada with optimism and joy in his heart. The explanation came from the lips of one of his fellow veterans as he addressed a television audience.

"We had a job to do, and we did it," he'd said. "The hope of happiness after the horror stayed strong in our hearts."

Perhaps memories of joyous Christmases had also played a part, the strains of Bing Crosby singing, "White Christmas" just barely audible through the roar of battle.

Christmas Labrador

Christmas can be a time of healing; a time for putting the pain of the past behind us and opening our hearts to new vistas of comfort and love. Such is the case in the following story of the Christmas Labrador...

This tale began one beautiful October afternoon, as I watched Ron securing the bottom of our chain link fence with tent pegs in another vain attempt to contain Brandy our wily Beagle, his dad arrived. After greeting his son, my father-in-law strolled over to join me.

"Ron always loved dogs," Wilson sighed as he sank into a lawn chair. "I guess all these fencing efforts are his way of trying to keep Brandy safe so your kids won't have to feel the way he did when Blackie was killed."

"Blackie?"

"The Black Lab mix he had when he was a little boy. One day when Ron was seven, Blackie wandered out of our yard and a neighbor shot him."

"No!" My breath gushed out in a horrified exhale. "That's terrible!"

"He never talked about it...not then, not ever that I know of." Ron's father squinted up into the sun. "I think it hurt too much. He loved that dog."

I didn't mention our conversation to Ron but that evening I came to a decision. Thirty years after Blackie's death, he deserved to have another wonderful canine; a purebred Labrador Retriever from the best bloodlines.

The next day I began my search for the perfect dog. Six weeks before Christmas I found exactly what I was looking for. Natalie Long of Acamac Kennels had been breeding championship-hunting Labs for over thirty years. After a lengthy telephone conversation with her, she and I agreed on a puppy fit for Ron, a yellow female named Daisy. Natalie assured me this dog had already shown an amazing aptitude as a hunter, one of the best she'd ever bred.

Even though I knew Blackie had been a black male, I remembered Ron had hunted contentedly over a yellow dog on more than one occasion. Daisy it was, I decided. The next day I sent a check off to Natalie Long. Only one problem remained. Natalie's kennel was situated three hundred miles from our home. *Oh, well*, I thought. *I'll figure something out.*

I'd planned to keep my gift a secret until a few days before Christmas but fate stepped in. The Canadian Armed Forces were offering tours of their facilities to a select group of secondary school teachers. Ron was chosen as a participant. The trip, by an amazing coincidence, would climax with a visit to the city nearest Acamac Kennels.

The temptation was too great. I told Ron about his present.

To say he was thrilled would be the understatement of the decade. His eyes rounded, he sucked in his breath. And then he kissed me as ardently as he had when we'd first started dating.

I must admit I did see a slight lessening of his enthusiasm when I explained his very own dream Lab was a yellow female but it was so minuscule, it barely gave me a moment's pause. In hindsight, I realize I'd been ridiculously naïve.

The next morning he set out on the tour, the agreement being that he'd visit his dog. By then, a plan that Daisy would be shipped to us a few days before Christmas had been put in place. Bringing her home ahead of time would not only be premature (we wanted to surprise the kids at an appropriate time) but also (I thought) impossible. Ron would be traveling by Armed Forces limo, no dogs allowed.

A week later I received a phone call. Ron had been to the kennel and he'd made a *minor* adjustment to my purchase. Instead of the five-month-old yellow female, he'd convinced Natalie to let him have a six-week-old black male. Furthermore, once he'd made his choice and held it in his arms, he refused to relinquish it.

"I'm going to convince the limo driver to let me bring him home with me," he said.

"But what about tonight? What about the no-dogs-allowed hotel you're staying at? What about milk? Isn't he too young to be away from his mother? Isn't…?" I sent a barrage of questions flying over the line.

"I've already smuggled him up to my room inside my jacket," he replied proudly. "I told a lady on the elevator it was my stomach acting up when he starting making noises."

"But food…?"

"I ordered warm milk from room service…for my upset stomach," my resourceful spouse replied smugly. "Tonight he'll sleep in the bed with me so he won't miss his mother and cry." He paused, then continued softly, shyly, "You'll like him. I named him Jet."

His words brought tears to my eyes. I didn't need a

thesaurus to understand his choice. No two color-based appellations could have been more closely related than Jet and Blackie.

"Good luck," I said.

I never knew how he did it but somehow he convinced his military driver to allow the puppy into the back seat of the big car. Consequently, the following afternoon Jet of Acamac the Third joined our family.

Several weeks later on Christmas morning neighbors dropped in. After the children had finished displaying their presents, Ron surprised our friends by proudly declaring his gift wasn't under the tree. It was outside...going to the bathroom (or some such euphemism) he declared proudly.

That night after the children were asleep and Jet lay curled up beside Brandy, the beagle, on the big dog bed next to the couch, Ron told me about Blackie for the first time. The Christmas Labrador had apparently worked one of those amazing occurrences for which the Yuletide is famous.

Jet's Gift

Although we had no way of knowing that Christmas when Jet first arrived to become part of our family, the big, gentle dog was to give us a greater gift than anything we could ever have imagined.

It began in the early autumn of Jet's first year.

Our twelve-year-old daughter Joan had just been diagnosed with a rare and potentially life-threatening blood disease. In the hospital, bruised and weak from transfusions, she'd begged for a day's reprieve to go to the country with her parents and her Black Lab pup, eleven-month-old Jet of Acamac the Third. After much deliberation, the doctor had agreed.

It was a gray September Sunday. Clouds hung low in a charcoal sky. We were packing to go home late in the afternoon when Jet, galloping joyfully after a squirrel, dashed into the path of an oncoming car. We heard tires squeal and the simultaneous screams from girl and dog.

When we reached the road, we found a deathly pale teenager kneeling in the ditch, an immobile pup clutched in her arms. A distressed motorist stood over them muttering, "I'm sorry. He ran right out in front of me. I couldn't stop in time. Is he alive? Will he be okay?"

Jet was breathing, but just barely. We gently wrapped him in quilts and loaded him into the back of our station wagon. Joan crouched in the hatchback, holding the dog's head, whispering words of love and encouragement.

Ron kept glancing into the rearview mirror as we drove toward the city. Each time our eyes met, I knew we were both wondering what would happen to our fragile daughter if she lost her friend. The doctor had warned us against exposing her to emotional stress.

Sunday has to be the worst day of the week to find a vet. Ours was no exception. He was out of town, his answering service informed us. If it was an emergency, we were to call his retired predecessor.

That veterinarian was a kindly old gentleman. He took one look at our pup and declared there was no hope.

"Have Tom put him down when he gets back tomorrow morning," he said sadly. "It'll be best. He's paralyzed."

Joan expressed no emotion at his words, but her blue eyes turned sapphire hard. Ron and I both knew that look. She wasn't about to accept the diagnosis, not without a fight.

We drove home in silence.

"Put him on my bed," Joan said when we arrived. Her tone allowed for no argument or refusal.

When the pup was laid as comfortable as possible in the center of her bed, I turned to her.

"Honey, it's only for tonight. Tomorrow…"

"I don't want to hear it!" she cried, throwing up her hands to cover her ears. Her arm hit her bedside lamp and sent it crashing to the floor.

In an instant, Jet was on his feet, staggering, falling over the edge of the bed onto the floor. Leaning against the wall, his eyes glazed with shock, pain, and confusion, tongue lolling out of his mouth, the big pup stared up at us.

"He's not paralyzed!" Joan was on her knees beside him, kissing him, tears rolling down her cheeks. "He's going to be all right, I know it!"

An hour later, she was still cradling Jet in her arms when I gently broached the subject of her return to the hospital.

"Let me talk to Dr. Henry," she said. "He'll understand. He'll know I have to stay with Jet tonight."

Ten minutes later, she handed the phone to me.

"He wants to talk to you," she said, then hurried back to be with her pup.

"I've decided to let her stay home tonight," the doctor informed me. "She'd never rest away from him. But bring her in tomorrow for a blood test. I'm concerned about how all this stress is affecting her condition. And let's keep our fingers crossed for the pup. She can't afford to lose him at this point."

That night, girl and dog slept in a tangle of quilts and pillows on the living room floor. Early in the morning, we eased the big pup from her arms and carried him out to the car. If he had to be put down, better to have it done before she was awake, before she had to say good-bye.

But our vet gave us wonderful news. After examining Jet, he told us he believed that with hospitalization and a lot of TLC, the pup could recover. How fully, Dr. Larsen couldn't be sure, but he believed the Lab deserved the chance to explore the possibilities.

Over the following months and years, the girl and her dog required much specialized care. There were lengthy periods of hospitalization for both. Jet lost part of one paw to infection and Joan needed multiple blood transfusions. Both had to take life much slower and more cautiously than the average girl and dog. But each time they beat their illnesses, life became just a little more precious to them. Struggling back to health, they were drawn inextricably closer in their quiet celebration of *joie de vivre*.

They even discovered there were plusses to their disabilities. At a reduced pace, they both had time to savor the hamburgers, to study the birds and flowers and bullfrogs along the way. Together they enjoyed summer showers, autumn sunsets, Christmas snowfall, and the first pussy willows of spring.

And what if one was a little too pale and the other walked with a limp? Their days were filled with the joy of lives bright with precious moments, moments they might never have been granted. He and Joan linked their spirits in a desire to survive

Jet even managed to give Dr. Larsen a kind of partial payment for saving his life. As a result of his constant and compassionate care of the chronically lame Lab, our vet was given an award by *Pets Magazine* for outstanding service to a patient.

But that wasn't Jet's only gift to the humans in his life. His courage and cheerfulness served as a daily lesson on how to celebrate life, no matter what its hardships. And while we were busy pretending he was no different than other dogs, Jet was just as busy forever etching his memory into our hearts.

When he died at age sixteen, Joan, a young teacher by then with her disease in remission, was heartbroken. For days, tears and a crippling sense of loss overwhelmed her. Then a sympathy card arrived from a friend.

"That which you have cherished with your heart you can never lose," it read.

Joan recognized the truth in those words. Stoically, she placed Jet's picture on her bedside table and found the strength to get on with her life.

She'd realized, like Ron and me, that although Jet was gone he'd never be forgotten. He'd been a joy and an inspiration all the days of his life. We can only and always be grateful that this wonderful dog shared our lives for so many years. The Christmas Labrador gave us a gift greater than anything we'd find under a tree.

The Chair

It's Christmas Eve as I sit alone in the living room in the chair. The rest of the family has gone to bed but I've remained behind, savoring the solitude as I watch the tree lights twinkle against the tinsel on its branches. The chair and I have shared so many memories....

The chair came from my maternal grandparents' house where it was part of the furniture they purchased in 1910 with this, their first and only home through fifty-three years of marriage. No one knows exactly how old the cane rocker was at that time but it probably dates from well before the opening of the 20th century. Its actual age means little to me.

What is important is the fact that at various times over the next fifteen years, it helped my grandmother rock all six of her children to sleep. And although she never talked about it, the chair probably cradled her within its arms as she mourned the loss of one of these little ones to diabetes in 1919 just two years before the life-saving discovery of insulin.

Years later, my mother and father were married in my grandparents' parlor with the chair as a silent witness. They moved into the big, old house with Granddad and Nanna the following week. Two years later I was born.

My mother told me she often rocked me to sleep in the chair although I can't recall the experience. Edited by the passing years I do, however, remember climbing up onto its worn cushions and snuggling down with my beloved stuffed dog, Fluffy. (No teddy bears for this youngster destined to grow into a world class canine fancier!) A book was invariably involved on those occasions, picture ones at first, later those of the story variety.

In those days, the big, old house was bursting at the seams with occupants as my uncles, one by one, brought home brides and settled in to await the day when they could afford homes of their own. Every square inch of space seemed to be in use, each mini-family assigned a single bedroom as their only private place.

This well-peopled household made for a bustling, festive atmosphere at Christmas. I loved the warmth and security a large, loving family offered at that special time of year. Most of my best memories of those wonderful occasions included the chair.

Each Yuletide I'd curl up in it to watch my grandmother trim the tree with small cardboard decorations she'd fashioned from discarded chocolate boxes and covered with the previous year's gift wrappings and ribbons. Aglow with the beauty and magic of it all, my child's heart overflowed with happiness.

After Christmas when the tree came down and the parlor once more returned to its deserted state, the chair became my sanctuary in the crowded household. The parlor, unheated to conserve fuel with its seldom-lighted fireplace and good furniture, offered a welcome retreat for an introverted child who communicated more satisfactorily with dogs than people, who passionately loved the written word, and who was content in her own company. To fend off winter's chill, I'd wrap Fluffy, the chair, and myself in a quilt and snuggled down to enjoy one of my ubiquitous books with only the ticking of the mantel clock for company.

Then, at age five, I made what for me was one of the best and most important accomplishments of my life in the chair. I LEARNED TO READ! Each afternoon, as soon as the dinner dishes had been washed, I'd beg my mother to come into the parlor, share the chair with me, and teach me the words that for her only daughter held all the magic and wonder of the universe.

She never refused. To this day, memories of my mother, Fluffy, and me stuffed into the chair with a book are among my most treasured.

When I was six my parents and I moved into our own home next door to my grandparents. My uncles also took their wives and went away. Granddad and Nanna used only a few rooms of the big, old house to conserve heat and maintenance. The chair remained empty and ignored in my grandparents' closed-up parlor. For a while even I forgot about it.

Then when I was eight, I decided I wanted to learn to play the piano. In our new home we didn't have one nor could we afford to purchase such a luxury. But in my grandparents' house across the backyard, in that closed-up parlor, was a perfectly lovely one. It sat right beside the chair. Shortly, with the chair an unfailingly attentive audience, I began to stumble over the scales and memorize the keys All Good Boys Deserve Fudge and FACE.

Producing aesthetically pleasing sounds soon proved to be an elusive goal for a child who couldn't carry a tune. Soon I abandoned the piano and returned to my first passion, reading, and what for me was its natural consequence, writing. The winter I was nine, curled up alone in the chair in the unheated parlor, my fingers pale from the cold, I wrote my first award-winning bit of literature…a nonsense poem that won first place in its division in a local elementary school contest.

That was all I needed. I was forever hooked. Writing would be my lifelong medium, my sanctuary, one of my major *raisons d'être*. I've always regarded this discovery as one of my life's greatest epiphanies. Discovering what you passionately want to do with your years on this planet can be nothing less.

But then life got even better. When I was twelve one of my fondest dreams was realized. At Christmas, I got a puppy. No more seducing neighbors' dogs into our backyard to play with me, no more stuffed imitations. I had an actual, living, breathing, chewing pet named Prince!

From the moment I first held his squirming little body in my arms, I knew one thing for certain. He and the chair had to meet.

Easier thought than done, I discovered that summer as I was heading across the dining room toward the parlor, my beloved puppy at my heels.

"You can't take that dog in there!" my grandmother's voice halted me. "He'll track in mud, he'll chew the furniture, he'll SHED!"

Not easily deterred (a basic characteristic for anyone with aspirations toward the writing life), I obeyed…for the moment. Prince and I returned to the backyard. I knew our time would come.

I waited only until my grandmother became

engrossed in her own passion, her rose garden. Then I gathered Prince into my arms and scuttled back inside the house, across the dining room, and into the quiet, late-afternoon hush of the parlor. Furtively so not to make a single squeak, we seated ourselves in the chair and settled back to enjoy my current choice of reading material, Jack London's *Call of the Wild.*

A feeling of utter fulfillment and happiness engulfed me as Prince and I rocked in the chair. It was as if all my dreams had finally come true. I was so absorbed in Buck's poignant plight I didn't hear the back door open.

When Prince started in my lap, I glanced up to see Nanna standing in the parlor doorway, a bouquet of pink roses in her arms.

I froze, guilt rendering me immobile. Never had I been so blatantly disobedient, so outright defiant of any of the adults in my life.

For seconds that seemed like hours Nanna and I stared at each other. Then she looked down at the thorny beauties in her arms, drew a deep breath, and turned away. Prince and I were never again denied access to the chair.

My next poignant memory of the chair comes from when I was fourteen and the boy who I'd thought was the love of my life jilted me for my supposedly best friend. My adolescent heart breaking, I huddled between the chair's cane arms with Prince and sobbed. The chair and Prince understood what parents and grandparents didn't. At fourteen a broken romance is the end of the world.

Five years later I did meet the love of my life. The day before I eloped with him I went into the parlor and said a thick-throated farewell to the chair. It understood I had to follow my heart even though I might never see it again.

The years passed. My sin of running away with the man I loved forgiven, I returned to the old house and watched my own children climb into the chair. Although now visibly aging, it welcomed them without a single groan.

More years passed. My grandparents and parents passed away. I returned to the old family home on each of these sad occasions and drew strength from the fact that the chair was still there, still a reassuring constant in my changing world. Each time I sat in it, I could feel its old, familiar sense of security envelop me.

Eventually my aunt inherited the old house and, of course, the chair. On a visit home, I was dismayed to discover she'd replaced the cane parlor furniture with a spanking new overstuffed couch and chair. The old rocker and its mates had been banished to the back attic over the wood shed.

I hesitated, then carefully broached the subject. Could I have the chair? I'd be happy to pay for it.

She also hesitated.

"Not right now," she said finally, carefully. "I want to keep it just a little longer."

I realized she shared memories with it, too. I understood and said no more about the chair.

Then abruptly, my aunt died. The house was to be sold, its contents divided between my brother and me. Aching from the loss of my beloved aunt, I didn't care about any of the modern new pieces with which she'd recently refurbished. I only wanted the chair with all its attached memories.

Then I discovered my brother had taken the chair to his house. Apparently my aunt had forgotten my asking for it and when she'd finally come to terms for parting with it, had given it to him.

Carefully I once more broached the subject of the chair with its owner.

"No problem," he replied immediately. "Take it."

Thirteen years my junior, he'd never lived in our grandparents' house and had never formed an attachment to the chair. Proudly, reverently, triumphantly, I carried it and its cornucopia of memories back to my home. The following year, curled up in the chair, I wrote my first award-winning book. Not surprisingly, it was about a dog.

These days the chair sits proudly in my own living room. Genteel, gracious, and welcoming, the chair is still my favorite place to write, my favorite place to dream, the very best place in this world for me to find myself.

And often late at night when I'm alone and sleepless and worried, I curl up in the chair, between its kindly old cane arms, and rock the pain and troubles into manageable heaps. It's my shelter in a storm, my comfort place, my reassurance that everything will turn out for the best.

I hope my children and grandchildren will find it in their hearts to keep the chair and cherish it for many years to come. I hope they will discover that the venerable old piece of furniture is much more than woven canes and faded brocade pillows. And I hope that on future Christmas eves, they'll find all the security, serenity, and inspiration between its ancient arms that I have. It will be a cherished part of my legacy to them.

Gail MacMillan

The Missing Windowsills

Windowsills, like the Yuletide season, have always sparked warm memories and held a magically special appeal. Decked out for the festive season, they brightened homes in the dark days of the winter solstice and provided a venue for the creative members of a family to display their talents. Sadly, as the years passed, broad window ledges that begged to be decorated in celebration of the season disappeared from architectural plans.

As a child living in my grandparents' Victorian home, I'd loved its venerable, cracked windowsills. Those dear old ledges had heralded the changing seasons as much as the first colored leaf of autumn or the premier robin of spring.

Late fall saw condensation gather along their inner ledge; in winter, it turned to ice; in spring, a puddle my grandmother mopped up with rags. In summer the cracked and peeling paint these changes had facilitated necessitated scraping and applying a refreshing coat that gleamed in the sunlight.

The windowsills' functions varied from season to season as well. In winter they became mini-greenhouses with pots of parsley, chives, and the like that provided fresh seasonings. In spring they held multiple small containers replete with earth and seeds in preparation for the growing season ahead.

Most memorably, each Christmas, before the commercial onslaught of outdoor lights and plastic decorations, my grandmother would decorate the wide sills of her bay window with Christmas cards from family and friends. These would be nestled among pine boughs trimmed with red ribbon salvaged from the previous year's gift-wrappings. Always the first part of the house to experience her talent for festive trimming, her decorated windowsills marked the advent of the Yuletide season for our family.

In other months my grandmother used her window ledges to display prized collections. Miniature porcelain cats, elephants, horses and even frogs were proudly placed where they could be enjoyed from both inside and outside her home.

Other windowsills throughout the house became places of safekeeping. Important objects were often deposited there.

"The keys are on the windowsill above the sink."

"I put the letter on the parlor windowsill."

"I left my wedding ring on the bathroom window ledge."

Beyond their uses in my grandparents' house, windowsills have proven inspirational to artists and photographers. I wonder how many pictures exist of cats hunched on these ledges, staring wide-eyed at birds beyond the glass or out into the rain or snow. And what about all those Victorian images of children and lovely young ladies leaning or seated on them, gazing wistfully outward as they waited for some person or event to put in an appearance.

This artistic fascination with windowsills carried over into fiction. Heroines leaned upon them as they waited for their lovers; villains pushed bricks, flowerpots, and other heavy, blunt objects off of them onto the heads of unsuspecting victims, and romantic heroes hoisted themselves over them in anticipation of eloping with their ladies fair. In musical ballads, bluebirds reputedly lit upon them as symbols of hope and joy.

On a personal level, who hasn't rested their elbows on a windowsill as they waited for someone or something to arrive? Who hasn't leaned over one to wave a fond farewell, perhaps even shedding a tear or two in the process? Windowsills have been involved in many emotional moments in our lives.

But, then, for a while, modern architecture all but eliminated these wonderful, multi-purpose catch-alls. In my first new home, it would have been difficult to place anything of interest or value on the minuscule edges provided in houses built in the latter part of the 20th century. Attempting to lean on one was out of the question.

But last summer, at our cottage, I experienced my own small architectural romantic revival. Our carpenter, installing a new double-casement window over our sink, created a windowsill! An actual six-inch-wide, flowerpot bearing, key-catching, knick-knack holding windowsill! Granted, I'd have to climb up into my sink to lean or sit on it but it's beautiful and nostalgic and inspiring just the same.

The varnish had barely dried when I placed a potted African violet on it and stood back to admire the effect. And although we don't usually spend Christmas at the cottage, I'm thinking I might just make a pilgrimage up there this December to trim that wonderful windowsill with pine boughs, red ribbons, and recycled Christmas cards.

The Case of the Telltale Sunbeam

The Christmas season in most households marks a time of vigorous tidying and cleaning, days and weeks when previously ignored nooks and crannies are ferreted out and denuded of accumulated dust and clutter. But try as any conscientious house keeper will, the first ray of sunlight to pierce the supposedly immaculate room will reveal dust motes dancing happily and unscathed in the supposedly pristine atmosphere. I'm sure such has been the case from time immemorial. Even the Holy Family, I can hazard a guess, was not spared these wily critters.

Images of Mary, Joseph, the Wise Men, shepherds, and animals gathered around the Christ child in the stable have always been among my cherished images of the Advent. The ray of light most depicters of the blessed event use to highlight the Holy Family is perhaps the most famous sunbeam (well, star beam but since stars are suns, let's not quibble) of all time. But even that divine ray must have revealed the dust particles and other floating allergens that hovered around the manger that blessed night. It had a lot in common with today's tattletales.

After the storm the week before Christmas, one of them had the audacity to slash into my den, a merciless home invader disguised as a golden beam. At first, slender as a sword's blade, it mushroomed until it encompassed a goodly portion of the room, careless of the havoc it was creating.

Dog hair appeared in profusion on the hardwood floor, nose and fingerprints became highlighted on the window, and a dried-up puddle (possibly piddle...I have three dogs) was revealed at the end of the couch.

I've never considered myself a super housekeeper but until that marauding sunbeam broke into my home I'd dared to consider myself a respectable one. Now, in a split second, I'd lost that distinction and a good deal of my homemaking confidence to boot.

Appalled, I rushed to clean in its wake. No amount of polishing or wiping or vacuuming seemed capable of eradicating the ray's carnage or the psychological damage it had done. I would never again feel safe from these heartless little luminaries.

All this may seem contradictory. I know most people regard sunbeams as positives...harbingers of the end of a storm, the dawning of a new day, etc. Who hasn't delighted in the delicate beauty of a sunbeam glinting through fresh greenery after a spring shower, highlighting the golden cornucopia of autumn, or bejeweling winter's snow-coated evergreens with an array of December diamonds. And how much nicer it is to awaken to a sunbeam tickling my eyes open than to be aroused by the harsh ringing of an alarm clock on an overcast morning.

Those bright little fellows have the power to lure me from my bed on even the most bitter winter morning. There's a special delight in discovering that warm place they've made on an otherwise cold floor and enjoying the magic they can perform by turning a frosty windowpane into a crystal kaleidoscope.

But the next morning when I got up and shuffled

into the bathroom to gaze into the mirror above the sink, a cruel companion to yesterday's thief lay in wait. Before I could turn a tap, this brutal beam splashed harsh reality over my face. I gasped. When did those laugh lines become so pronounced and the dark circles under my eyes become bags? Most alarming, when had my adorable dimples become the centre of a rippling lake of wrinkles?

The kitchen offered no relief. More of the bright miscreants lay in wait there, ready to showcase the crumbs on the counter, the fingerprints on the fridge and microwave. Another boldly allowed dust motes to dance along its length in a bright diagonal that stretched across the entire room. Suddenly I knew exactly how Pig Pen of Charlie Brown fame feels.

An hour later I climbed into my car and heaved a sigh of relief, confident I'd left the sunbeam carnage behind. Until I reached up to adjust the rear view mirror.

The sound that emanated from my throat found a definitive description in the word "squawk."

There, invading what I'd believed to be the sanctity of my car, was another one. Hitting me squarely in the face, boldly assaulting me with my reflection, the pillager shredded the last of my self-confidence as he flashed across my mouth to reveal plum lipstick bleeding down previously invisible pucker lines.

Infamous little beggar!

As I backed out of the drive and headed off up the street, I struggled to regain my equilibrium. I would not be undone by anything as insubstantial as a few small light rays I told myself and began to formulate a defense. Perhaps I could find some excuse to confine my chauffeuring duties to overcast days. That way, I'd be alone when those brazen hooligans invaded and no one would witness the cruel truths they delighted in hurling across my physiognomy.

And since I couldn't stop their coming, I could at least sunbeam-proof my home. The next time the doorbell rings, I'll scuttle across my living room and close the drapes, then rush into the kitchen and bathroom to pull the blinds. Guests may think I'm living in Dracula's closet but I'll have foiled those marauding little devils and limited their quest for uncompromising reality.

I wonder how Mary felt about that beam of long ago. Glaring down onto her precious babe, did it wake the Holy Child? Did it make her aware of the dust-filled conditions into which he'd been borne?

Ah, sunbeams. Trouble makers in a guise of gold but still evokers of Christmas memories.

Santa's Revised Schedule

Of course, no memories of the Yuletide would be complete without recalling the traditions of the Jolly Old Elf. Santa Claus arrives on Christmas Eve sometime after all good children are fast asleep in their beds. While visions of remote control toys and digital doodads dance through their heads, Santa slides down the chimney or, in lieu of such an opening, through a convenient door or window. He sorts through his sack, finds the appropriate gifts, and deposits them under the tree. He pauses only long enough to eat the snack left for him, lay a thoughtful finger aside his nose, give a nod, and then it's off to the next house.

But did you know Santa can and will adjust his schedule to fit special situations? He will. I know. Over the years I've had two experiences with his flexibility.

The first, of course, was the famous verandah roof landing. For years, that lovely little story remained in the realm of my memory. Then, one Christmas after Ron and I had become the parents of three preschoolers, I told him about Granddad's intervention with Santa. The story inspired him.

What if *we* asked Santa to come early on Christmas Eve? That way Joan, Carol, and Steve could get the much-anticipated gifts before going to bed, thus ensuring all of us a decent night's sleep. We wouldn't be roused at 5:30 a.m. to see what Santa had brought.

Of course, there was still the matter of giving Santa privacy to do his good deeds. Ron again had a solution. The whole family would go for a drive to enjoy the neighbors' lights and decorations after supper on Christmas Eve. We'd let Santa know the house would be uninhabited and that he was welcome to drop in during that time slot.

Santa co-operated. Over the years he penciled the MacMillan house into his schedule between 8:00 and 9:00 p.m. each Christmas Eve. He even paused long enough to drink the milk and eat the cookies Steve never failed to leave for him. Ron said he sometimes added a piece of fruitcake and a napkin when he had to go back into the house while we waited in the car. It seemed every year he forgot to check the woodstove or turn out some of the lights or lock the back door.

Santa's revised schedule became a welcome tradition in our family, something our children would remember vividly and with as much fondness as I remember those alleged hoof prints on my Granddad's roof.

Gifts Awry

"Mom, there I was, stark naked except for a towel! And all because of your Christmas gift!"

Hands clutched tightly to her hips as she described the results of my present, my twenty-year-old daughter stood in my office doorway a week after Christmas. Although I didn't immediately catch the significance of the event, later I'd realize that here yet again was another incident that would be added to my collection of Yuletide remembrances.

"But the gift certificate was supposed to be for a facial," I defended my good intentions. "Of course, there was just a tiny language problem…the sales lady didn't speak very much English…and I thought it was rather expensive."

"For a facial, yes. For a complete body massage, no."

So much for Good Intention Number One I thought a bit ruefully after she'd gone. Oh, well, one down, three to go. My other unique gifts *had to be* hits with their recipients.

My burst of originality occurred several Christmases ago when, struck by a sudden desire to give absolutely unforgettable gifts, I had abandoned my usual offerings of sweaters, socks, books, and chocolates.

I started my quest with my eldest daughter. For over a year, she'd been longing to have a facial but being a university student, the treatment was beyond her financial means. So *viola*! A gift certificate from one at the most exclusive spas in town. Unfortunately, there'd apparently been some sort of mix-up, a minor misunderstanding, and so, the above scene had occurred one morning early in January.

I heaved a sigh as Joan left my office and comforted myself that my other one-off gifts had to meet with more success. I felt a nice, warm glow as I thought of the present I'd given to second daughter, nineteen-year-old Carol.

As a child, Carol had longed for a pony, then a horse, then riding lessons. Since none of these had been financially possible at the time, I'd determined that now, at least part of her dream should come true. A week before Christmas, I called a local stable and signed her up for a series of riding lessons.

But once again, misadventure was to dog my best intentions.

"Mom, the horse laid down! The minute I got onto its back, it laid down!" Carol's voice reached new heights in decibels when she called me from the riding academy. "Then it jumped to its feet and took off like a bat out of you-know-where! My entire life flashed in front of my eyes! I thought I was going to die!"

No, no, no! Horses don't fall down, then leap up into full flight.

"Perhaps you've put on some weight, dear, and that's why he fell down," I countered lamely. "It is just after Christmas and all those goodies..."

"I don't think so, Mom," my 119-pound daughter replied sarcastically.

Ah, well, *c'est la vive*. Carol had had a taste of her

dream and survived to tell about it. My description of an adventure. Two gifts down and two certain-to-be-a-hit ones left to go.

Autumn came. The leaves tumbled to the ground but not my optimism. My husband, as usual, geared up for duck hunting season. This year he was especially well-equipped right down to a brand new (if a bit green-trained) retriever and an extraordinary safety device I'd given him for Christmas.

Basically it was a flashlight but it also contained a siren and a flashing police-type light to be snapped on in case of emergency…a wonderful device for a man who had the frequent (and unnerving for me) habit of hunting alone. Pushing the memory of the results of my previous two Christmas debacles aside, I watched him drive off on the first day of the season, dog and light beside him, a satisfied little smile on my lips.

"I may as well have taken a brass band!" my husband exploded a trifle incoherently when he returned that night.

When I was finally able to draw articulate speech from him, the appallingly amazing story came out in a rush.

Apparently the new (and green) aforesaid canine had managed to dart ahead of him as he was sneaking stealthily into his duck blind. Stumbling, my husband had simultaneously pushed two buttons forward on that remarkable safety device. Instantly siren and flashing lights had exploded into action.

Ducks had risen screaming into the clear morning sky for "miles around." A poacher who'd been hiding nearby had fled past the unfortunate pair, apparently convinced that the entire local detachment of RCMP was closing in on him.

At this point, I admit becoming a tad discouraged with my gift ideas. Then I remembered what I'd given my son. And panicked. He'd recently left Banff, Alberta to drive back home to the Maritimes. I'd given him a compass-watch to facilitate his journey. He'd left four days previous. Would I shortly be getting a call from Yellowknife or Dallas to say that gift, too, had proven an adventure?

"Mom." I held my breath as I recognized my son's voice on the phone.

"Hi, Steve." I paused, then ventured, "Where are you?"

"At the New Brunswick border," he replied cheerfully. "I'll be home in a couple of hours. The compass-watch works great…even gives a pretty accurate ETA. See you soon, Mom. And thanks."

I hung up the phone, a small sigh of vindication and relief easing from my lips. One out of four isn't that bad I tried to console myself. But the following Christmas, I reverted to sweaters, socks, books, and chocolates. Just to be on the safe side.

Enough with this kind of memory making!

It's the Christmas Beagle, Charlie Brown!

Christmas is a season of mysterious, often miraculous events. At least that's how I've come to explain the arrival of a new and totally unexpected family member several Yuletides ago.

I can't deny my part in the event. After all, this newcomer is a beagle and I do love those small rascals of the hound type. I can't help it. Oh, I know they can be stubborn, hedonistic, exasperating, with an insatiable penchant to chase anything that moves and unrelentingly single-minded when it comes to getting their own way.

They can also be funny, clever, loving, and totally endearing. These characteristics, in my opinion, make up for all of the preceding.

They're free thinkers, the Bohemians of the canine kingdom. Hippies that came to England with William the Conqueror, they've been spreading their doctrine of enjoying life to the fullest ever since.

In modern times, beagles have inspired books and movies such as "Shiloh" and classic cartoons featuring the one and only Snoopy. Then, of course, there's Kristin Von Kriesler's moving book *For Bea, the Beagle Who Changed My Life*.

A beagle changed my life as well. His name was Brandy. For more than sixteen years he inspired me, humbled me, amused me, horrified me, and loved me all in his own inimitable way.

When Brandy first became a member of our family, I was a fledgling writer with a single not-best-selling novel to my credit. In fact, I purchased Brandy with the last of the meager advance I'd received for that book. We'd just lost our beloved dog, a beagle-mix named Ben. My children were grief-stricken. In an attempt to alleviate their sorrow, I said I'd find them a beagle puppy.

At the time I'd never known a single purebred beagle outside of the cartoon Snoopy and had absolutely no knowledge of the unique, free-spirited being that lurked within the little tri-colored body. Or of the devilish Machiavellian brain that functioned between those gorgeous velvety ears.

I soon found out.

By the time he was three years old, Brandy had escaped my custody with sufficient frequency to have stolen food from most of our neighbors and chased their cats and horses to distraction. He'd disappeared for hours at a time in pursuit of rabbits (or any other wildlife he could startle into flight) and streaked through picnic dinners and weak-sided camping tents, apparently unconcerned about the chaos he created.

He'd also stayed by my side during the most excruciatingly painful illness of my life and inspired me to begin a series of dog articles that later appeared in magazines from coast to coast both in the United States and Canada. Ultimately his death would prompt me to write an award-winning biography of his incredible life and develop a deep and abiding concern for beagle welfare worldwide.

When he passed away at the ripe old age of sixteen, I was left with a vast, unquenchable sense of pain and loss. I vowed that never again would I allow a beagle to entrench itself so deeply in my heart.

Then, several Christmases ago, my daughter Joan and I volunteered to clean pens at the local SPCA. These kind people had just taken in two dozen refugees from a terrible puppy mill. Among them were several beagles.

As I cleaned pens and refilled bowls, I tried to ignore the little hounds. Getting involved with them would only serve to stir up memories I wanted left alone. As I glanced in their direction and saw them leaping nearly to the top of the two-and-a-half meter-high pens, I knew they would be the hardest of the rescued dogs to place in good homes. It's not everyone or every household that's able to deal with a beagle's high-spirited, free-wheeling exuberance.

One beagle in particular, I felt certain, would have trouble finding a proper placement. She'd been confined in a lobster trap for the first nine months of her life. As she'd grown, she'd never been able to walk or even stand up. A bloody hole in her side bore bitter testament to where the cage's steel had pierced her body. Of all the dogs that had survived that puppy mill, she'd suffered the most. No wonder she was especially wild. Even the limited freedom of her pen must have seemed like heaven to her.

This basic lack of restriction must have inspired her. Two days previous, in a bid for even wider vistas, she'd managed to scramble over the top of her pen in the night. When the SPCA caregivers had arrived for work early the following morning, they'd found her sitting happily amid the utter chaos of overturned shelves and scattered supplies, tail wagging, eyes bright and eager.

Now she was chained inside her cage, front paws

braced against the wire, white-tipped tail wagging furiously as, head thrown back, she howled out her beagle cries above all the others. God help the kind soul who takes her on I sighed inwardly as I went to empty my bucket.

When I returned to the kennel area minutes later, I froze. I couldn't believe what I was seeing. My daughter sat on the floor of *that* beagle's pen, the little hound cradled in her arms as it licked her face with joyous abandon.

"This is my dog, Mom," she said softly.

This couldn't be happening. Joan had always been a Labrador retriever fancier. In fact, we'd recently been surfing the web for breeders. Now, here she sat, holding one of the wildest beagles I'd ever encountered in her arms and declaring it hers.

Something miraculous in tune with the Christmas season must have overwhelmed me. The following morning I found myself signing a joint adoption agreement that would give me shared responsibility with Joan for this, the wildest of beagles. The deal was I'd keep her during the day while Joan, a principal at a rural school, was at work.

I could barely believe that another beagle was coming into my life as suddenly and as unexpectedly as that. Had Brandy, in his deviously relentless way, gotten through to me via my compassionate daughter? Was it perhaps his way of telling me it was time to move on, to share my life with another happy-go-lucky adventurer of his ilk? Perhaps Brandy, as he always had, was forcing me on to new experiences and, in doing so, to remember him with each hair-brained adventure into which this new beagle would take me.

Or maybe it was just one of those inexplicably wondrous events that have a way of occurring at Christmas. Who knows? One can never be sure when dealing with a beagle.

Joan named her Scout after Harper Lee's memorable "To Kill a Mockingbird" character. Scout accompanies me to book signings and poses for pictures with as much perky enthusiasm as if it was her biography, not Brandy's, she's touting. Once again I've been seduced by beagle charms. I even managed to laugh the day she leaped aboard my tea wagon and rode it, skateboard fashion, across the living room.

And each time I watch her racing full-speed around the perimeter of our fenced backyard, ears streaming out behind her head, wild with exhilaration in this semblance of freedom, I share the fullness of her delight and rejoice in it.

Of course, she will chase anything that she can urge into flight and follow her nose into one incredible (and often dangerous) situation after another, but after each cavalier exploit, she climbs up onto my lap to plant a big, wet beagle kiss on my nose and snuggle close, the celebration of life that is the spirit of Christmas glowing from her heart.

The Pug Who Came to Dinner

This Christmas story has its beginning at our cottage in Tabusintac one beautiful evening in June last year. When I opened the door to call our dogs…Molly, the Nova Scotia Duck Tolling Retriever, and Barbie-Q, the little no-name brand…for dinner, I recognized him immediately. New neighbors had moved in across the road two days earlier, and the Pug was part of their family. I'd seen him playing on the deck of their cottage. He looked up at me, big brown eyes round and appealing above the black mask that covered his snout, and wiggled his curly pig-tail.

Beside me, Molly paused and looked up. I knew that expression. I glanced over at the neighbor's cottage. No one was around.

"Okay," I answered Molly's silent request. I looked down at the Pug. "Would you like to stay to dinner?" He wriggled his tail again, than pranced up the steps and past me.

He proved to be an appreciative guest, his enjoyment of our doggy cuisine obvious as he burrowed his little black mouth deep into gravy-laced kibble. He even gave a lusty burp and licked his chops with gusto when he finished.

"Bruiser! Bruiser, where are you?"

He cocked his head on one side, then trotted to the full-length screen door and looked out, tail wiggling. His reaction left no doubt. He *was* Bruiser.

I opened the door for him and followed him onto the deck.

"He's over here," I called across the lane to the young woman in shorts and tank top. "He stayed to dinner."

"Thanks." She jogged across the road as Bruiser rushed to greet her. She introduced herself as Nancy as she lifted his squirming body into her arms.

"Bruiser's an unusual name for a Pug," I said, as she tucked him against her side.

"I named him after the dog in the movie 'Legally Blonde'," she grinned. "Hope he wasn't any trouble." She waved and headed back across the road carrying the Pug.

"Any time," I called.

The trouble began the next morning when Molly dashed out as usual to fetch the morning paper at the end of the drive. At the corner of our cedar hedge where the carrier normally tossed it, she stopped short. No paper.

She lowered her nose and began a serious investigation of the area. After a few minutes of watching my dog's unsuccessful attempts to find the daily news, I scuffled into my moccasins and went to help her.

As I was opening the front door, I saw my new neighbor running across the road in slippers and PJs. She was waving something in a blue plastic sleeve. Under her left arm, Bruiser hung ignominiously.

"Sorry," she said as she ran up the steps. "Bruiser's been watching your dog fetch the paper for the last couple of days. He must have thought it was a good idea, so he brought your paper to us."

"No problem," I replied taking the paper and giving Bruiser a little head-pat. "Shows initiative, right, guy?" He licked my hand, snuffled a Pug sound and wriggled his tail.

It's been said you can't outfox a fox. Molly soon proved that the cliché also applied to Nova Scotia Duck Tolling Retrievers. Bright and early the next morning, she posted herself on our front step. As I glanced out the front window, I saw a small, black-masked snout peering out from the hedge.

I got my coffee and drew up a chair. This was going to be interesting.

A few minutes later, the carrier's car appeared over the crest of the knoll on the road above the cottage. Molly leaped to her paws, alert and ready. Half hidden behind cedar branches, a small amber fawn critter also came to attention.

The car slowed at the end of our drive, an arm appeared through its open driver's window, and the morning news flew through the air. Simultaneously (or so it appeared) both dogs lunged.

The collision occurred at the corner of the hedge. A yelp, a squeal and Bruiser was sent catapulting backwards into the bushes. Molly paused, glanced disdainfully at her competition, then picked up the paper and trotted back to the cottage, head held high; the obvious winner in this war for words.

Bruiser had scrambled to his paws. He shook himself, paused a moment (I assume to make sure he was still intact), then proceeded to prance behind Molly toward our cottage.

When I opened the screen door for Molly and accepted the paper she carefully presented "to hand,"

Bruiser, his *joie de vivre* apparently unabashed, trotted inside behind her, the corners of his mouth curled up in a good-natured grin.

The following morning, it bucketed rain and Molly opted to watch for the paper from the front window. Surely, she may have speculated, the Pug wouldn't come out in such inclement weather for a fetch he must now know he couldn't possibly hope to retrieve.

Molly would soon learn never to underestimate the tenacity of a Pug.

I'd gone back into the kitchen for a moment when I heard the carrier's car approaching, and Molly's excited whines.

"No rush, girl," I assured her as I headed toward the front door to let the now yelping, prancing dog out.

Then I saw the reason for her distress. Bruiser had darted out of the hedge and lifted his leg. His aim perfect, he peed on her precious blue-sleeved paper.

Two weeks later, Nancy crossed the road to ask a favor. She and her partner were going to visit non-dog-fancying relatives for a couple of weeks. Could we keep Bruiser?

No problem Ron and I agreed. By then Bruiser had become a frequent and welcome visitor. Barbie-Q and Molly enjoyed him, and so did we. So the Pug who came to dinner gathered up his collar, leash, and bowl and moved in.

"He's housebroken and doesn't chew things," Nancy said as she placed him on the kitchen floor. "There are only a couple of tiny problems. He steals and he parties."

"Oh?" we replied in surprised unison although the former came as no surprise after the newspaper incidents. But as for partying… A Pug? Really!

The first couple of days nothing untoward occurred. The three dogs played happily on the deck, in the yard, and at the beach.

On the third morning things changed.

When I went to call the dogs in after their morning ablutions, I found a pair of pink plastic flowers, a few of their fake petals missing, on the deck. I recalled having seen them on a neighbor's lawn. Bruiser sat beside them, a grin plastered across his pushed-up little face.

"Did you take those?" I asked pointing to the purloined posies. "No, No! Bad boy!"

The black ears drooped repentantly for a moment. Then he blinked an eye at me and wiggled his tail.

An hour later, when our neighbor went grocery shopping, I furtively stuck the two worse-for-wear flowers back in her faux-flower garden. That was easy I thought as I trotted home. And now that he knew better, our houseguest wouldn't do it again. He'd looked so contrite.

Apparently I hadn't learned anything about Bruiser's persistence during his paper-pirate days I realized later that week. Each morning our deck sported new booty. A tennis ball, a toy truck, a plastic shovel, a baseball cap, a deflated beach ball (I refused to reflect on how it had gotten into that condition) and, most alarmingly, what looked like a doll's amputated arm.

Worse was yet to come. The next morning, a shoe appeared on the deck. Obviously new, obviously expensive.

"Oh, Bruiser!" I breathed, turning the slender, high-heeled strappy sandal over in my hands. "What have you done now!"

For a moment, my tone of voice made his ears droop and his tail straighten. For a moment he looked almost ashamed. Almost. And only for a moment. Then, his tail re-knotted, his ears went up and his mouth widened in that now-familiar roguish grin.

Ron joined me on the deck. "There's only one thing to do about this," he said. He took the shoe from my hand and, like the prince in Cinderella, set off down the road to find someone with its mate.

"That's it." On his return, Ron picked up the Pug and looked him squarely in the eyes. "No more stealing, understood?"

For a moment, black ears drooped and the broad mouth sagged. For a moment one could almost believe he was truly sorry. Almost.

The instant Ron replaced the canine culprit on the deck, his entire body flashed back to perky exuberance. He turned to Barbie-Q who'd been dozing in the sun and began racing around her, barking and daring her to play.

"When did Nancy say she'd be back?" Ron asked as the two little dogs made circuit after circuit, barking and yelping.

That evening marked the beginning of a long weekend in New Brunswick. Shortly after 6 pm, the air grew rich with the smell of barbecuing beef and pork from our neighbors' barbeques. All three dogs, lying on the deck, bellies full of supper, sniffed deeply. Leaving them to savor the aroma, I went inside to clear away our dishes.

I returned to the deck twenty minutes later to discover Bruiser missing. When 9:00 pm arrived and he still hadn't returned, I set out to look for him. Yes, most of our neighbors informed me, he'd visited their parties but he was no longer around. Finally, as darkness and mosquitoes gathered around me, I headed home. I hoped to find him on the deck. No such luck.

When the rest of our household settled to sleep ("He'll be along," Ron said confidently as he headed off to bed) I curled up on the couch with a book to wait...

I awoke with a start when I heard paws on the deck. Stumbling to my feet, I switched on the outdoor light. There stood Bruiser, a big T-bone thick with meat clamped in his jaws.

"Where have you been?" I scolded opening the door for him.

He glanced up at me disdainfully, then staggered up the steps and past me into the cottage, clutching his booty. He reeked of fat and barbecue sauce.

He looked up at me again, gave a weary sigh, then headed for the kitchen. There, with a tired grunt, he climbed onto the couch that had become his bed at our house. It took the last of his energy to bury his loot under a pillow. The task completed, he settled himself on top of it and closed his eyes. His belly, bloated with the results of foraging from party to party, stuck out from beneath him.

Nancy arrived home several days later. With big news. And a request. She'd decided to join the armed forces. Could we keep Bruiser while she was away at boot camp and basic training?

"Well...okay," we agreed.

For some reason, Molly chose that moment to demonstrate a trick I'd been trying to teach her for several days.

She lay down on the deck and covered both eyes with her paws.

Bruiser, sitting beside her, grinned.

But the story doesn't end there. After all, where's the Christmas bit, right?

Nancy returned from boot camp at the end of her training and collected the Pug. We watched him go, knowing she was taking him to Vancouver and that our chances of ever seeing him again were slim to none. That night I shed more than a few tears after the rest of the family had gone to bed.

The following spring Nancy again contacted us. She was being deployed on an eight month mission. Would we take Bruiser once again?

He arrived on a cold day in April with his suitcase full of food, toys, bowls, collars, leashes, and even a warm winter coat. As Nancy deposited him on our living room floor, he looked up at us grinning the broadest Pug grin ever and swirling his curly tail so fast I thought it would be launched free of his little backside. He had returned and was glad of it.

We had a great summer with Bruiser as part of the family but as November approached and time for him once again to leave us approached, I felt a lump in my throat every time visions of the impending separation came to mind. He'd been with us so long this time, had become so much a part of our family. I began my Christmas shopping but with no real enthusiasm. Whenever anyone asked me what I wanted, I stifled the urge to tell the truth: that I wanted Bruiser to stay forever.

And then the call came. Nancy had arrived back in port in Vancouver and would be coming to New Brunswick the week before Christmas. I told her Bruiser was fine, that he was fit and ready to go but the ache behind my eyes was a painful sting that held back tears. We talked and joked and then we hung up, and I cried.

Two days before Christmas I got another call from Nancy. She was being deployed at the end of January. Her voice broke as she made the request. Could we keep Bruiser permanently? Shipping him coast to coast each time she went to sea wasn't fair to the little guy. He deserved a permanent home with people who loved him. She knew we were those people.

Joy burst over me like a skyrocket. Yes, of course. We'd adopt Bruiser and care for him and love him, and Nancy could visit whenever she had an opportunity.

So two days before Christmas and many years after that Yuletide when I'd wished so vehemently for my first dog, I got yet another. Apparently the magic of the season is still intact and going strong.

Hands Remembered

My father's hands frightened me as he tried to hang the tiny chocolate box ornament on the Christmas tree. Once my source of strength and reassurance, they trembled and fumbled. I couldn't bear to watch. Those same shaking hands had fashioned many of my best memories. Now there'd be no more and all because of a disease called Parkinson's.

My thoughts went back to those Sunday afternoons when I'd been a teenager and totally enamored with horses.

"Step here," my father would say holding down his big, cupped hand.

Obediently I'd place my booted foot into the human stirrup and rise, phoenix-like, upwards until I could scramble into the old cavalry saddle strapped to the back of my grandfather's Percheron. I took the strength in my father's hands for granted.

Those same hands were also capable of great gentleness. When I was suffering from a severe case of food poisoning he sat by my bed all through that fearful night, dipping a face cloth into a basin of cool water beside my bed, wringing it out and wiping my fevered forehead time and time again until the brunt of the illness had passed. My father was a mechanic by trade, and I can still recall the scent of motor oil from his damp hands that night. To this day the smell of automobile lubricant brings a warm feeling of reassurance wafting over me.

My father's hands supported me when he was teaching me to swim and ride a bike. I slipped into the water and onto the seat of my first vehicle confident he'd keep me safe.

That sense of confidence inspired by the touch of my father's hands extended into other facets of my life. Most winter Sunday afternoons, from the time I was nine or ten, my father and I would don skates and head up the brook that led away from my grandfather's farm and into the woods beyond. We'd skate far back into the forest only turning back when the long shadows of a winter's dusk began to darken the way.

As the shadows spread and thickened and an owl hooted in the encroaching gloom, I'd skate closer to my father, closer and closer, until his gloved hand stretched out to me. I'd clasp it in my mitten and know I was safe from any dangers the night forest might hold.

In junior high school I suddenly became ashamed of my father's oil-stained hands and broken fingernails. I didn't want my friends whose fathers worked in offices and banks and hospitals to see his laborer's hands. I didn't stop to remember the strength and kindness in them or the food, clothing, and shelter they'd amply supplied for my mother and me for so many years.

He must have recognized my embarrassment and quietly absented himself whenever I brought friends home. I'm still ashamed of how I treated this loving, gentle man during those selfish days of adolescence.

I became a woman, married, and left my father's house for several years. When I returned I brought a baby daughter with me. With my husband, her biological father, working five hundred miles away, Joan at fifteen months readily accepted her now widower grandfather as a surrogate dad.

He delighted in the role. Even after a long day's work at his service station, he always found the time and energy to push her proudly up and down our street in her stroller.

One night I awoke to find my father seated on a chair beside Joan's crib in my room. He had a basin of water and a face cloth and was bathing her small face. He'd heard her crying and had come into our room to discover her running a fever. Pregnant with her sister, I must have been too deep in sleep to hear her distress.

As I sat up a sense of *déjà vu* wafted over me. Those same work worn, gentle hands, now wrinkled and knotted with age were just as kind and capable as they'd ever been.

Years later when he was diagnosed with Parkinson's disease my heart ached as I watched him struggle to sign his name or drink a cup of tea. He could no longer hold a book or newspaper steady enough to read. When he had to give up his job and forfeit his driver's license, he'd wilted.

Eventually he developed pneumonia and lapsed into a coma. He couldn't speak and his eyes were closed by the time I arrived at his hospital bedside. I pulled a chair as close to him as possible and took one of his hands between mine.

It felt so cold and limp, looked so white and clean that at first it seemed as if I was holding the hand of a stranger.

"Daddy," I whispered. "I'm here."

Pale fingers struggled and moved in mine.

For the next two days I sat by his bed, holding his hand and reminiscing, letting him know how very much I'd appreciated him and what beautiful and poignant memories I had of our years together. Once in a while, getting weaker and less frequent, his fingers would stir in mine, and I'd know he was still listening and understood.

My father passed away quietly one November afternoon as I sat by his hospital bed reminiscing about our time together. I hope in those last hours of his life I was able to return at least a small measure of the strength, courage, and love his hands had always given to me.

Although physically he's no longer with me, I know that he's never far away in spirit. Whenever I'm distressed or frightened or tired, I can still feel his hand on my forehead, gentle and strong and reassuring and smelling of motor oil.

Of Mice and Memories

One frosty, overcast Christmas Eve I returned to the camp. It had been thirty years since I'd visited the place but that morning I'd felt a sudden, intense need to revive its memories. As I entered the overgrown space that had been its firebreak, a carrion crow rose into the cold, gray sky, its cries raw and blasphemous in the reverent hush. An icy sense of loss washed over me.

All that was left among the tangled undergrowth was a pile of rotting gray boards. Even the Star stove that had been the old building's heart was only a bit of rusted cast iron with lids missing and oven door hanging on a single hinge. A small animal had built a nest inside. A mouse perhaps? I remembered mice...

Thirty years ago hunting camps built by my father and his friends had been veritable mouse hostelries. Single-roomed creations of boards nailed to two by fours, roofs tar papered to keep out rain and snow, these cabins had never experienced the luxury of caulking. The process hadn't been deemed necessary by their hardy inhabitants. The resultant cracks and crevices offered natural invitations to small rodents.

The old camp that had once stood in this clearing had, over the years successfully withstood the assaults of larger, more threatening visitors. With its plank door scarred by several attempted porcupine burglaries and an area beneath its rear window gouged by a marauding bear, this particular camp had been a place I preferred to stay inside after nightfall.

But, of course, even there wildlife (mice) abounded. One night after we had retired to bed, I heard my father muttering from the bunk beneath mine.

"What is it?" I asked struggling to get comfortable on the planks that served as box spring and mattress.

"Darn mouse keeps running over my face," he replied.

His words drove all possibility of sleep from my mind at the speed of light. While I have never been unreasonably leery of sow bears with cubs or cow moose with calves, the vision of an insomniac mouse galloping across my head still has the ability to render me sleepless on any given night.

On another night, when a group of my father's friends joined us in the camp for a late evening feast of partridge stew, the mouse again put in an appearance. Or perhaps I should say appearances. In the flickering light of the oil lamps, he kept darting devil-may-care across a rafter directly over the stove where the uncovered pot of stew sat simmering. His shadow was immensely grotesque on the plank walls, and I assumed I would not sleep again that night.

But when my father and his friends began telling stories, my obsession with the mouse temporarily ceased. As the fire crackled and snapped and boots and socks huddled up to its warmth to dry, these old-time hunters spun yarns of the best of hunts and the worst of hunts; about well-remembered gun dogs including the farm Collie that had once treed a cougar and of a high-bred, much touted Spaniel so timid he'd piddle at the mere sight of a shotgun. And of other nights in other camps when, on one occasion, my father claimed he'd found black peas in the rabbit stew.

Only when the tales came to an end did I realize I had lost sight of the mouse. When I glanced up at the beam, he was gone.

"That mouse won't bother you tonight," one of my father's droll guests caught my glance and grinned. "He slipped off the beam and fell into the stew."

But in recompense for the mouse, there were those wonderful nights when rain thundered across the tar papered roof. Warm and dry in my sleeping bag, my jacket rolled into a pillow beneath my head, I don't believe I have ever felt as content…

Awakening in the pitch darkness to the pattering of the first shy droplets, I would roll over onto my back, fasten my fingers beneath my head, and settle down to enjoy nature's symphony as it built to a thunderous crescendo. On such nights, even the mouse seemed to be lulled into foregoing his nocturnal ramblings.

Later, soothed by the rhythm of the rain, I'd sleep. In the morning I'd awake to a golden dawn as sunlight slanted through the ripening October leaves dripping crystal droplets outside the window. As my father scraped back the lid of the old wood stove to start the breakfast fire, the finale of the night's water music would be slipping from eves and trees.

Later we'd feast on sausages, eggs, and bread toasted over the fire washed down with several steaming cups of strong tea. Then we'd head out to hunt the freshly washed autumn bush.

As we walked away on one such morning, our boots swishing though the wet, encroaching undergrowth, I paused and looked back at the camp. Alone beneath lofty pines, maples, and birches, it was growing gray and gaunt.

From the left wall of its weather-bitten façade, the stove pipe elbowed its way outside, then right-angled up into the brisk morning air. Half way along its length a bit of support wire had been looped about its girth and tacked to the roof near the peak. A drizzle of smoke from our dying breakfast fire drifted drowsily skyward from its rusting mouth.

The previous spring my father had fastened a piece of window screening over the opening in an effort to keep sparks in and small forest creatures (mice) out. His work, it appeared, had been at least half in vain. On the rain soaked doorstep, my anathema, the mouse dry as the proverbial bone from a night no doubt spent indoors, sat sunning himself in a blade of sunlight that had sliced its way into the little clearing through the living canopy of greens and golds.

Suddenly the entire clearing appeared bathed in soft tungsten light, a mellowing bit of the almost-past that could not come again. I shivered, pulled my collar up against the early morning chill, and turned away. I was nineteen and about to leave my father for another man…the man I was to marry…

Three decades later, on this Christmas Eve, I knew I shouldn't have returned. My father had died three weeks earlier, a victim of unhappiness and Parkinson's disease. I wished I could remember him only as he'd been in the days before my mother's death, a failed second marriage, and a debilitating illness had ravished his unique sense of humor and *joie de vivre*. Before he and the camp had become destined for this sad, quiet end.

Thirty years. In the encroaching dusk, I eased the

sagging door of the stove shut a little more to keep out the weather. Maybe that nesting mouse was a descendant of the one that *hadn't fallen* into the stew that night many years ago.

I wanted to protect him. He and the old camp had joined the ranks of precious Christmas memories.

A Place of Peace

Christmas and its cards bring images of beautifully bucolic little churches nestled in the snow. For our family and especially for my father, these images have been poignant reminders of St. Stephens.

It was natural that his most beloved place of worship was pastoral St. Stephen's. My father always found peace and spiritual renewal in nature. He saw God in a summer's sunset, the first pussy willows of spring, autumn's golden glow, and winter's silent purity.

Established on a small island in Black River in northeastern New Brunswick nearly 170 years ago, St. Stephen's has remained isolated from the bustle of daily life. The little country church, surrounded by lofty maples and venerable pines, has continued to be what it has been since its beginnings…a place of peace.

With its ambiance of reverend tranquility, St. Stephen's has drawn our family to worship for nearly two centuries. Over the years, five generations of my ancestors have formed a generous portion of its congregation.

At any given time, its choir has consisted at least in half of our relatives. One of my aunts (great-great, etc.) usually played the organ. In the days before electricity came to the little community one of my ancestral uncles manned the bellows that provided its power. My great-great uncle James preached there briefly in the

1850's…until his free thinking made him unpopular and he felt compelled to move on. (Later he would become the first professor of Natural Science at Queen's University.) We still have our own special pew in St. Stephen's. The stained glass window my great grandmother donated in memory of my great grandfather stretches upward above it.

This window was installed in the second building that became St. Stephen's. Scottish settlers built the original structure in 1836. Among them was my great, great grandfather George Fowlie from Aberdeenshire. That original church building housed the small, rural congregation until shortly after the advent of the 20th century. By that time, it had fallen into disrepair and the congregation thought it wisest to replace it with an entirely new structure, the present day St. Stephen's.

My earliest memory of the second St. Stephen's embodies standing beside my six-foot, three-inch father when I was five years old, awkwardly sharing a hymnbook with the man towering above me. A lower section of the family stained glass window had been opened to let in the July breeze. Sunlight streamed in through the remainder of the closed panes, making rainbows in the dust motes floating in the air. Each time we reseated ourselves after a song of praise, the old, much-varnished pews would creak kindly, a sound as familiarly reassuring as the voice of an old friend.

Like a trusted old friend, St. Stephen's always put my father at ease. A shy man who found the big town church with its finer trappings and more formal atmosphere intimidating, he felt at home in the little church on the island. He and I attended services there in all seasons. In summer, through open windows, bird song and gently rustling leaves accompanied the sermon. Sometimes a seasonal storm bucketed rain down the steep roof and lightning flashed. In fall we made our way up its steps over a carpet of golden leaves. In winter, this changed to a blanket of snow. In spring, at Easter, the island's burgeoning pussy willows proved and welcomed nature's revival.

My father drew strength from the little church's intimacy with nature and felt inspired by it. Certainly the tales he told me reflected a deep kinship with the old church. A gifted storyteller, he always spoke of St. Stephen's with a kindly affection usually reserved for a trusted companion with whom he'd shared some of the best moments of his life.

One of my favorites involved the church's Christmas tree. In the days before electricity reached the little church on the island, real candles illuminated the boughs of the fir brought inside for seasonal celebrations.

"Your uncles and I were given the task of manning the water buckets kept near the tree in case it caught fire," I remember my father telling me with a grin. "And it usually did. For young fellows our age, dousing that burning tree became the highlight of our Christmas Eve."

My father saw nothing sacrilegious in their enjoyment of the event. The God he met at St. Stephen's had a sense of humor and understood young boys.

Christmas Eve gatherings were only one of the many events held at St. Stephen's. In the days before television or even radio intruded on the peaceful rural community, the church served as a community center. My father told me stories of frosty sleigh rides to attend a Sunday evening youth group called Christian Endeavour. Lucky lads often got to see their favorite girl home afterwards.

And then there were the basket socials where the men of the congregation bid on lunches prepared by their wives and sweethearts (or, hopefully, their future sweethearts). I recall my father telling me about one such event when he and his brother were both interested in the same young lady. During the course of the evening, my father managed to switch her basket with his sister's. As a result, his brother ended up sharing the picnic supper with his sister while my father enjoyed the meal with his heart's desire. Again, he was sure God chuckled.

Perhaps the most endearing story my father told me about St. Stephen's took place during another courtship, when he was dating my mother. Justifiably proud of his community's beautiful little church, he took her to services there one fine autumn Sunday evening. As usual, one of my uncles controlled the bellows that powered the pump organ.

This process later was a source of amusement for me whenever, as a child, I became bored with the service. Each time we stood to sing another hymn, I'd watch, fascinated, as the top of one of my father's six foot plus brothers' head would pop up and down behind the screen designed to hide shorter human sources of power from the congregation. I often played a little game in which I tried to guess which of my uncles was at the pump that day. On the evening my father took my mother to his church for the first time, my Uncle William manned the bellows.

"That sermon never seemed to end," I recall my

father telling me. "Every time I thought he'd finished, he'd start up again."

When it finally did conclude and the choir got up to sing the last hymn, the congregation quickly followed suit. My aunt at the organ brought her fingers to the keys with gusto to play the opening bars.

Nothing happened. Absolute silence filled the little church.

She tried again. Still nothing.

With a mutter of disgust, my father recognized the problem and leaped to his feet. Chagrined before the lady he was trying to impress, he strode out of the church, around its side and into the small space behind the pulpit that housed the organ's source of power. With all the passion of a knight-errant, my father thrust aside his sleeping brother and took to the bellows.

A great gust of air gushed into the organ all but lifting my startled aunt off her seat at the keyboard.

His brash actions must have impressed his lady love. The following September, he and my mother were married. Years later they were laid to rest together in the serenity of St. Stephen's cemetery.

Whenever I need to talk to my father, I only have to walk into that peaceful place and stand beside his grave. Amid the soft music of the breeze soughing through the pines and maples, I know he'll always be there for me.

At Christmas when I visit St. Stephens and gaze at it snuggled in the virgin white of the season beneath snow frosted pines sparkling in winter sunlight, I find the same sense of serenity that he did. It never fails to help my heart find the true spirit of Christmas once again.

The Enduring Christmas Wish

Christmas is a time for wishing. Some wishes are attainable; others we recognize, even as we make them, as being in the realm of fantasy. One of my most cherished ones fell into the latter category. Learning to ride a horse and having one of my very own went right to the top of my wish list when I was five and fell in love with a photographer's pony.

I recall falling hopelessly in love with its soft, brown eyes and velvet nose. Oh, how I longed to scramble onto its chubby back, even for a few seconds, to fun my fingers through its wiry, black-and-white mane, and pat its sturdy neck.

My mother didn't approve of those people who went door to door leading a sleepy-looking Shetland pony and offering to take children's pictures on its back. Therefore, I didn't get the brief, momentary thrill of being placed in its saddle that day. Denied the opportunity, the incident left an unquenched longing in my soul.

That year at Christmas I squeezed my eyes shut as tight as I could and wished and wished. It didn't work.

Over the years, my maternal grandfather, a life-long horse fancier himself, would indulge my wish as best he could by taking me to pony rides at the local county fair. He'd stand patiently by the rail while I circled the ring time and time again on a bored, plodding pony, fantasies of cantering across a field full of daisies dancing through my head.

When I reached the age of twelve and became too big for the pony circuit, my paternal grandfather allowed me to saddle up one of his Percherons and ride, always well within his view, at a sedate walk or shambling trot up and down the lane behind his barn.

Neither of my grandfathers' kindnesses could fully quench my desire to ride a real saddle horse of my very own. Consequently each Christmas I continued to wish.

Through my teen years, I managed a few trail rides at local stables and even a couple of riding lessons from a neighbor who owned a lofty hunter. Brief and transitory, these equine encounters failed to satisfy my desire for a personal bonding with one special mount.

Marriage and children followed and I shelved my dream. I had a wonderful family; to ask for more from life would have been greedy. Nevertheless each Wednesday when our weekly newspaper arrived, I read an ad offering riding lessons at a nearby stable. Each Wednesday I'd fantasize about having the time and money to indulge myself without the faintest belief it could ever be possible. My canter across that field of daisies would remain a fantasy.

But when Christmas rolled around, I still couldn't resist wishing.

Years passed. Children grew up and graduated from university. Money became less of an issue. But by then, I was nearly fifty, too old to achieve my dream. Or so I thought.

"I think it's time you took those riding lessons you've always wanted," daughter Joan startled me by suggesting one Saturday morning. "I've called the number in that ad you've been reading for years. They can fit you in this afternoon."

I tried to protest. I was old enough to be a grandmother. It was too late. My words fell on deaf ears. Joan bundled me into her car and off we went.

Someone once said (I think it might have been Winston Churchill) that the outside of a horse is good for the inside of a man (or in this case, a woman). He was right. From the moment I first scrambled aboard my mount, Dee, I discovered a new world. Stress, fatigue, and old-fashioned depression vanished immediately. Nothing could match a good, long ride in fresh, country air. Even when it was raining. Even if it was at a shambling walk.

Dee, like myself, didn't mind the rain. In fact, she seemed to prefer a silver-cool morning to hot, fly-infested bluebird days. I'd let her shuffle to a walk as we turned down a trail into the trees. Dee at nineteen, an equine equivalent to my own age, felt no need to hurry. Trained from filly-hood to the familiar Western Pleasure gaits of walk, trot, and lope she could make these transitions as smooth as good milk chocolate.

In an effort to bring myself up to speed with Dee's superior knowledge, I took riding lessons from her owners and became the bane of their existence by proving no great prospect for the next Olympic Equestrian team or even a winner at the local pony club show. I didn't care. My absolute pleasure in spending time with Dee overshadowed my lack of skill. As kind and gentle with me as she was with the ten-year-old who'd learned balance and coordination on her back the previous summer, Dee only looked puzzled the day I led her from the barn, her saddle tilted to one side, one ear flattened under an improperly positioned bridle strap.

The tolerant mare taught me how to keep the bit straight when I put it into her mouth and told me with a shake of her head when I pulled the girth too tight too fast. She waited patiently as I climbed aboard and then steadied my wobbly body with the rhythm of her even gaits.

That autumn the stable owner asked me if I'd like to lease Dee. She knew I wasn't in a position to buy the mare and take her from the property. With the lease, Dee would be my horse exclusively while remaining at the stable for care.

I was ecstatic. After decades of longing for a horse of my very own, I'd finally achieved my dream. Oh, I've never succeeded in cantering across a field of daisies...a faulty sense of balance has never allowed me to speed, steer, and stay in place all at the same time. But each morning when this fifty-something lady saddles up and heads out, she knows dreams can come true.

These days, each Christmas I give thanks for the magic of a season that can keep a dream alive for forty-five years.

Lassie Never Did Come Home

My dogs, with their unconditional love, boundless *joie de vivre*, and eternal optimism have always showed my heart the way to the true spirit of Christmas. They've shared my good times and bad and never once faltered in their love for me or their belief that I will do the right thing.

Through the years, over a dozen dogs have shared my life and brightened my days. This past year, four monikered stockings hang from our mantel this Christmas. They read, left to right, Molly, Bruiser, Scout, and Barbie-Q. Curled up on the rug in front of them are the four canine characters for which they've been monogrammed; a Nova Scotia Duck Tolling Retriever, a Pug, a Beagle, and a little no-name brand.

In my wildest dreams I could never have imagined this mixed four-pack all those years ago when I first began wishing with all my heart and soul for a dog, any dog, just as long as it had four legs and barked. Nor could have I imagined my Christmas wish would eventually lead to over a dozen dogs a-barking instead of the twelve drummers drumming that the lyrics of "The Twelve Days of Christmas" promised.

I was twelve when I'd finally managed by blatant trickery to get my first puppy on the Christmas of the China Dog. Like Agatha Christie who was so overwhelmed with delight on being presented with her first dog she ran away and hid, I could barely contain my joy. When Prince finally left me to cross the rainbow bridge, I thought the pain of his passing would never subside.

For a few years I remained dog-free, not able to once again give my "heart to a dog to tear." Then, shortly after my marriage, Ron, knowing my love for all things canine, found a dog, a Samoyed husky whose owner was terminally ill and desperately seeking a good permanent home for his beloved dog. We were living in an old farm house in the country at the time and had room for a big dog.

When Ron arrived home with Star in tow, I instantly broke my vow about never again giving my heart to a dog. A Samoyed husky was still a very long way from the Collie of my dreams but Star was a wonderful dog, she needed a place to live, and we had room both in our hearts and our home. Little did we realize then that this would become a pattern for our lives.

Later Ron would adopt Smokey, a lovely Yellow Lab. A gentle giant who loved our children as toddlers and accepted small hands pulling his fur as each struggled to their feet to make their first steps. Smokey exhibited nothing but love during his days with us. When a job placement forced us to move to the city, Smokey remained to live with friends on a nearby farm. A small urban apartment wouldn't have been a fair or decent place for a large dog who loved country freedom.

Three years later I took our seven-year-old son to the local SPCA to look at dogs. I kept reminding Steve that we were "just looking." Although we'd recently bought our own home with a yard and might possibly be able to manage a dog, the time just didn't seem right. As we were leaving the shelter, I noticed Steve clutching his jacket that seemed to be quivering independent of my son's movements. I understood a moment later when a tiny puppy head appeared near the neckline.

"This little dog needs a place to live." My son looked up at me. His tone and expression brooked no refusal.

We went back inside, paid for the puppy, and signed the necessary adoption papers. Twenty minutes later Ben, a beagle mix, was on his way home with us, unplanned but definitely not unwelcome.

Sadly Ben ran away from our cottage one summer day two years later and was struck by a car. All three of our children were devastated especially Carol, the middle child. To placate her tears I promised we'd get a beagle puppy…a breed about which I knew absolutely nothing except that they definitely were not Lassie-type dogs.

Three weeks later Brandy a purebred beagle joined our family. The following Christmas Jet a Black Lab arrived to companion him. For the next sixteen years, Brandy led us through a series of adventures, some of which would have made James Bond cringe. Jet watched from the sidelines, good naturedly wagging his tail and taking it all in his stride. I remember looking at them more than a few times over that decade and a half and thinking there were few pairs of dogs that could be further from my dream Collie.

But what the heck! They were great dogs and everyone in the family loved them. Those are the most important ingredients to a satisfying human-canine relationship.

One day when both our dogs were well into the double digit years of their lives, I saw an article in a magazine article about Nova Scotia Duck Tolling Retrievers. At last here was a dog that appeared tailor made for me. Over the years I'd felt my need for a Collie diminishing as I became more and more enamored with retrievers. But these little red dogs had somewhat the look of a Collie combined with the wonderful temperament of a retriever.

My first loyalty was to the two wonderful senior dogs that had been living with us for over fifteen years. Certainly no dog or puppy no matter how perfect could ever take their place.

Brandy passed away just before his seventeenth birthday. My heart ached and burned. He'd been my beloved (if often bohemian) friend for so many years. It was months before I could even consider inviting another dog to come live with us.

But finally spring and renewed hope arrived. In reading a dog magazine I came across the name of a breeder of Nova Scotia Duck Tolling Retrievers. I hesitated. Would calling that breeder and inquiring about a pup be disloyal to Brandy's memory? It took a lot of soul searching until I finally decided Bran, with his love of life, would want me, while keeping him safely in my heart, to get on with mine.

Later that summer my *very first actually selected* dog arrived. Harbourlights Highland Chance was beautiful, vivacious, clever and gregarious. Here, at last, was the dog of my dreams.

Two years later Jet, who had never fully gotten over the death of his life-long beagle companion, passed away. As a result of this sad event, there was room in our home for another dog. Pleased with Chance, I called her breeder for yet another NSDTR, but this time I was looking for a mature dog. Chance, a lovely dog in maturity, had been a hell raiser as a pup as she attempted to devour the toes of every family member.

The dog the breeder sent this time was Chance's half-sister, a lovely three-year-old named Ceilidh that had been returned to her birth kennel when her owner, a naval officer, had gone back to sea. She'd been obedience trained, housebroken, and seemed absolutely perfect. Except for one outstanding problem. For the rest of her life, she would suffer severe separation anxiety.

Chance, on the other hand, appeared flawless. Not that she was loved or respected any more than the rest. It was just that she was the chosen one who turned out to be the perfect show dog, the excellent hunter, the amazing companion. She went high in trial in every show of a two-day Canadian Kennel Club event and two days later headed out to the marsh to attract and retrieve a hunter's limit of ducks. The following week she worked as a therapy dog at a veteran's home and posed for a number of magazine photos. She was definitely destined for canine stardom.

Sadly fate was about to step solidly and unrelentingly into our lives. The trend began one day in early September when we returned to our cottage the year Chance turned six. There we found a surprise. Under our barbecue, shivering in the cold rain, was a very tiny mixed breed puppy. Unassuming and totally charming, the little waif immediately captured our hearts. We never in our wildest dreams expected to have three dogs but this little one asked so little, offered such a heart-full of unconditional love that we couldn't give her up. We named her Barbie-Q.

Two weeks later Chance began to act strangely. She'd climb into our bed each night, panting, slapping at us with her paw. We thought she was simply jealous of Barbie-Q and told her to be a good girl.

We couldn't have been more wrong. Two weeks later Harbourlights Highland Chance CD jumped off the couch at our cottage and died. The shock was overwhelming. One minute we had a beautiful, vibrant dog and the next moment a small red corpse.

I couldn't allow an autopsy. I was too broken hearted. We would always accept her passing to be the result of a heart attack.

In recompense, Barbie-Q reached out to us in our sorrow, climbing onto our laps and offering all the comfort one small heart swelling with love could offer. In retrospect, I believe Barbie-Q was sent to us in preparation for our losing our too perfect, too wonderful Chance. I cannot imagine how we would have gotten through the shock and the aftermath of Chance's death without Barbie-Q.

In the wake of the tragedy, Ceilidh also surprised us by suddenly opening her heart to the little orphaned puppy and adopting her as her very own. Although she would remain mostly aloof with us for the rest of her life, she'd found something of her very own to love and nurture in Barbie-Q. It brought her out of her shell of loneliness and gave the little foundling the mother she so badly needed.

We mourned Chance all that winter but by now we'd learned that what we'd cherished in our hearts we could never truly lose. By spring we were able to move on and Nova Scotia Duck Tolling Retriever puppy

Molly joined our family. Molly was a sweet, quiet little girl who immediately became Barbie-Q's best friend and Ceilidh's second puppy. The job of mothering two active pups took up so much of Ceilidh's time I think a good deal of her initial homesickness fell by the wayside.

Six years later Ceilidh left us to join Chance. Her two puppies, now wonderful dogs, stood solemnly by her grave. It would be a long time before they saw their surrogate mother again.

The following Christmas our daughter Joan and I jointly adopted a beagle that had been much abused in a puppy mill. Scout, as Joan named her, although milder than Brandy, nevertheless was pure beagle in personality. She quickly became a source of joy as well as astonishment on numerous occasions.

Five years later Bruiser a Pug whose "mother" in the military could no longer keep him joined our family. He and Barbie-Q quickly became a couple, a couple of canine culprits I nicknamed them, four-legged Bonnie and Clyde's as they traveled around our neighborhood at the cottage in summertime, raiding other dogs' kennels for bones.

This Christmas our yearly card bears the images of these four very different dogs, only one bearing a resemblance to the dream dog I wished for all those Christmas's ago. Molly the Nova Scotia Duck Tolling Retriever sits on one end overseeing her strange little pack of three; Barbie-Q, Scout the Beagle, and Bruiser the Pug. I love them all dearly but as I watch them sitting in the bay window in front of the Christmas tree I can't help thinking of the old saying, "Be careful what you wish."

When I first wished so fervently for a dog I never envisioned over a dozen dogs a-barking their way through my life. I've never had a single moment of regret that Lassie never did come home. Each and every one of them have kept the unconditional love and eternal optimism that is a goodly part of the Christmas spirit glowing in my heart not just at the Yuletide but all year long.

Invisible Gifts

Last Christmas I received a wonderful gift from my grandfather who'd passed away twenty-five years ago. It was in the form of an inspiration for a story. It didn't surprise me. It was only another in a long series of intangible presents I've received from family members, living and deceased, over many years.

From my paternal grandfather I received a love and respect for all creatures great and small. His farm where no form of cruelty or disrespect toward animals was tolerated provided lifelong benchmarks for me as an appropriate level of caring for all God's creatures. Later in my life, this perception would emerge in a series of magazine articles on animal care and three dog books.

My paternal grandmother, dying young before I had the opportunity to know her, gave me an insatiable curiosity about my ancestors and, indeed, all those who had gone before. This interest in the past would eventually manifest itself in my researching and writing a number of historical pieces for magazines and two history books.

From my maternal grandfather, I received a passion for the detective story. He introduced me to Erle Stanley Gardner, Dashiel Hammett, Agatha Christie, and Rex Stout when most children my age were devouring Nancy Drew and the Hardy Boys. These days, with five mystery novels to my credit, I'm grateful that he did.

His remarkable wife presented me with a fascination for romance and adventure. As a child I listened enthralled as she conjured up memories of Victorian ballrooms where elegant, high-collared gentlemen gallantly signed the dance cards of beautifully gowned young ladies to gain the brief pleasure of their company in a waltz or quadrille before they marched off to fight in a foreign war. These images still have the power to spark my creativity and fuel my imagination at a moment's notice.

My mother gifted me with a passion for the printed word. She read to me every day from the time I was born until I had mastered the skill for myself. I remember her leaving dishes in a sudsy pan when, at age four, I stood behind her pulling at her dress, book in hand, and begging, "Please, just one chapter. Just one chapter." A devoted amateur actress, she read with verve and emphasis and forever instilled in me the magic to be found on the printed page.

From my father I received a love of poetry and the outdoors. A man with an eighth grade education, he taught me to see the beauty in a summer sunrise, an autumn resplendent in red and gold, a winter's day magnificent in virgin white, and how to set it all into descriptive blank verse. He found his strength and religion in nature, truth, and beauty and taught me to do the same.

My husband has given me four decades of commitment, of being there when I faltered, of believing in me when I no longer believed in myself. He's partnered me in my writing career, letting my fads and fancies lead the way. I've seen exasperation and bewilderment mirrored in his face from time to time but never doubt. There definitely must have been times he's wondered exactly what I was up to, where this new scheme was going but he's never once questioned my judgment. It can't always have been easy.

My children have brought me pride in their achievements, in the strength of their characters, and, most of all, in their many acts of kindness that reach well beyond the realm of family and friends. I've seen them unobtrusively slide change across a supermarket check-out counter when the person ahead of them comes up short. I've watched them adopt abandoned animals, bury fallen sparrows, and stand up for what they believed against daunting odds. I've seen their compassion for the less fortunate and less lovable in our society and marveled at the genuineness of their sense of equality for all. This world will truly be a better place because they passed this way. What better gift could a mother receive? Their altruism has formed the basis of a goodly number of my stories.

Thank you, everyone! And Merry Christmas!

A word about the author...

Award winning author of 32 published books, a graduate of Queen's University, Gail has had articles and short studies published throughout North America and Western Europe.

Visit her at:

macgail@nbnet.nb.ca

Other titles by Gail MacMillan
available at The Wild Rose Press, Inc.

Heather for a Highlander
Counterfeit Cowboy
Rogue's Revenge
Shadows of Love
Holding Off for a Hero
Ghost of Winters Past
Caledonian Privateer
Lady and the Beast
Highland Harry